I'M TIMMY

A Novel by
T. S. Kincaid

Copy ©2024 T.S. Kincaid

1ST Edition

This story is a work of fiction. Names, characters, organizations. places, events, and incidents are either products of the author's imagination or are used fictiously. Any resemblence to actual persons. Living or dead , is entirely coincidental. No part of this book may be reproduced or stored in a retrieval system, or transmitted in any form or by any means, electronic, mechanical, photocopying, recording or otherwise, without the expressed written permission of the author.

ISBN: 979-8-9914681-0-7

Cover Design @asthetic_Adeel

I'M TIMMY

Hallwick & McIntire
Copy ©2024 T.S. Kincaid

A Novel by
T.S. Kincaid
Book One in the Timmy Series

To contact the author go to

TSKincaid.com

I would like to dedicate this book to my

dear friend and mentor

Sandra McIntire

I would also like to dedicate this book to

my sister and best friend

Sherry Murphy

Thank you both for always being there

Love, T.S. Kincaid

"It was love that kept us here." She explained, "But people like that don't know what love is. They did things a purpose. They *meant* to harm people. It weren't like an accident or that they just did things from negligence. They was evil. And they have done other things that showed how mean and evil they really was. Nope, people like that don't get a choice. They go straight to hell."

Klara

Chapter 1

I STOOD LAST in line, not wantin' to get on bus 247. Other kids got behind me but I let 'em cut the line. It wasn't that I didn't wanna go home... I did. It's just that I thought maybe *they* was on the bus, and I didn't want to see 'em. Not today.

T. S. Kincaid

I seen my shadow movin' back and forth, rockin' like a rockin' chair when the wind blows and ain't nobody in it. I like to rock. It makes me feel better, but daddy always touches my shoulder and says, "Timmy, stop bubby, you're rockin' again."

The line was gettin' shorter. My chest started feelin' funny like my heart was gonna jump out and run away without me. It was poundin' so loud I was sure Mary Jo, the girl in front of me, could hear it.

Someone jerked my hand from my mouth and said, "Timothy Thomson! That is a filthy, nasty habit young man! Not only should your hands be kept to yourself, but also out of your mouth!"

It was one of the teachers from third grade. She 'bout scared me to death! She musta been subin' for Mr. Jeters, 'cause I heared he'd been out sick that day. Anyways, I looked down at my bleedin' fingertips. My nails was so short they looked like little stubs.

"Yes ma'am," I said.

Sweat rolled down my back. It was so hot and that stinkin' bus was makin' me sick. I tripped on my stupid shoelace and fell into the bus, hittin' my leg on the hard, metal step. The bus door squeaked closed behind me.

I crossed my fingers and whispered, "Oh please, don't let 'em be here today."

I'M TIMMY

I walked slow, checkin' each seat. I stretched my neck as far as I could when it happened. I seen 'em. Hunched down, hidin' near the back of the bus. I uncrossed my fingers as they came climbin' over the seats, one in front of and the other behind me. The meanest boys I ever seen, Eddie and Beau Rogers. I knew now that this day, like all the others, was gonna be a long, scary ride home.

It started with Eddie sayin', "Monkey in the Middle," and grabbing the tattered comic book outta my back pocket. Beau grabbed it and threw it back to Eddie as I tried to get it. Eddie held it behind him just out of my reach. They both laughed each time I thought I almost had it.

I was so mad. I could feel my face burnin'.

Finally, I stomped and yelled, "Ggggive it back, or I'm ttt-ellin'!"

Beau looked at his brother and said, "Uh, tattlin' must run in the family."

Eddie had a funny look on his face, shook his head, and said, "Oh, yeah!"

He looked at me with his beady eyes. His face was pinched like someone squeezed it together, and it got stuck that way. Then he said, "Like father, like son."

I had no idea what they was talkin' 'bout.

"Go ahead, tttattle-tell, Tttimmy, I dare you!"

Boy! That did it! I was so boilin' mad! So, I had a hard time sayin' things sometimes, so what? My fingers curled into a fist. I guess Beau seen 'em 'cause 'fore I knowed it, he had his fists up. He opened his hand, and his fingers told me come on.

My eyes started waterin'. Every time I get mad, I cry. I tried to wipe my tears away, but they was too fast and ran down my cheek.

Eddie busted out laughin'. He pointed his dirty finger at me and started singin' "Cry-baby, cry-baby, Tim-my is a cry-baby."

He took my comic and acted like the leader of a band wavin' a stick around, gettin' all the other kids to join him. I looked over at Mary Jo. At first, she just sat there, but then she started laughin' and yellin' it too. I felt so bad; I thought she was my friend. Alls I could do was hang my head.

At first, I liked Eddie and Beau. They seemed real nice when they came to our yard on their bicycles. Mama and daddy and me'd just moved to Raymond, and the boys always wanted me to come play with 'em.

I'M TIMMY

Daddy'd shake his head and say, "No, not today, bubby."

One day, after they'd gone, I was feeling kinda brave and I asked daddy why I couldn't play with 'em. I was so lonely and I wanted a friend so bad.

Alls he said was, "Those boys are too old for you, Timmy. They're mean and up to no good."

He was right, too. After what I seen, I never wanted to play with 'em again. I guess really, that was when all the trouble started.

It was a Saturday, and the birds chirpin' outside my opened winda woke me up. I lay there listenin', tryin' to figure out what kinda birds they was. My Mawmaw Pike tried to teach me the different sounds they made when we lived with her in Frankfort. That was the capitol of Kentucky. We learned that last week in school, but I already knowed that 'cause we'd lived there.

Anyways, I thought I heard a robin, but when I looked out the winda I was wrong. It was a bluejay. Darn, I really thought I had it that time. I guess I forgot. There was so many birds she tried to teach me 'bout. Maybe I was just too little then. After all, I am almost seven and a half now. I bet if she was here now, I'd know 'em.

I miss her.

What was I sayin'? Oh, yeah, the trouble with Eddie and Beau.

Well, I was layin' there listenin' to the birds when I heard the toilet flush and the water runnin' in the bathroom. Then, heavy footsteps was comin' down the hall. I closed my eyes real tight when my door squeaked open.

Daddy said, "Hey bubby, you 'wake?"

I pretended I was 'sleep and let out a loud snore.

"Oh," Daddy said, "I guess you're still sleepin'. I was gonna go to the park 'fore I head out to work today, but, oh well."

I threw those sheets off me so fast they looked like a big fluffy cloud floatin' down from the sky.

"Do ya really mean it, Daddy? Can we really go to the park today?"

"Absolutely. Get dressed, and I'll fix you some cereal."

The walk to the park was swell. Have you ever seen how the leaves make different shadows on the ground when the sun shines through the trees? Well, I like to

I'm Timmy

play hide-and-seek with the sun and see if I can jump from shadow to shadow before the wind blows the branches and makes the pattern change. Daddy walked behind until we got to the swings. I asked him to push me.

"Come on, Timmy, you're a big boy now, big enough to swing yourself."

"Please, Daddy," I begged.

He grabbed my ankles and lifted me high above his head. And then he ran underneath and I flew up into the air. My belly dropped on the way back down.

"Oh wow!" I screamed. "That was the highest I've ever been. I felt like I was flyin'."

Daddy smiled as he walked over to the bench and sat down. He lit a cigarette and blew perfect circles of smoke outta his mouth. I loved when he did that. I liked to break the rings like I was poppin' bubbles. But not this time. I was havin' too much fun swingin'.

Then I seen the lady with the dog. I love dogs. I always wanted one. I dragged the front of my shoe on the ground to slow down, back and forth, 'til I finally stopped. And I ran up to the lady.

"Easy, Timmy," Daddy said. "You don't know that dog, and he's liable to bite."

"Oh, she's very friendly," said the lady. "She won't bite. Would ya like to pet her?"

"You bet!" I said.

I slowly put my hand out, and her soft tongue licked me. I kneeled down closer, and she put her paws on my knee, lickin' my face. It felt funny, and I laughed. Her eyes were so sweet. She was small, but not too little and her fur was the color of my hair, yella. Her eyes were brown, just like mine.

"See? She likes you."

"I like her, too," I said.

"Well, guess what? She's gonna have puppies. Would you like one when they're old enough to leave her?"

"Would I?" My smile was so wide it hurt my cheeks.

"Whoa, whoa, whoa, there, Timmy." Daddy said, 'you know how your mama feels about animals. You know she'd never allow it."

My smile turned into a pout.

"Well, maybe we could change her mind?" I asked, puttin' on my saddest face.

"I don't think so, bubby, sorry."

I'M TIMMY

My heart sank until the woman said, "Hey, maybe you can still play with 'em when they get bigger, and I bring 'em to the park. Would ya like that?"

"I sure would," I smiled.

A gray squirrel ran from a tree and down the hill to the next. The little dog barked and took off the fastest I've ever seen over the hill after it.

"Sheba! Get back here!" The woman yelled as she took off after her. I started runnin' with her, but Daddy said, "Timmy, we don't have much time. You'd better stay here and play while ya can."

"It'll be alright," the woman said, "She does this all the time, those dern squirrels." And off she went. I could hear her yellin', "SHE- BA! SHE-BA!" As she went down over the hill. She came back a few minutes later, but there was no Sheba.

"You still didn't find her?" Daddy asked.

"No." The woman said, "but knowin' her, she's probably already gone home."

"Well, we'll keep a look out for her," Daddy said.

"Thanks," said the lady as she walked off. She yelled for that little dog 'til I couldn't hear her no more.

I kept playin' a little longer. First on the merry-go-round, then the jungle gym, and finally the big shiny slide. I won't lie; when I got to the top of that slide, it sure did look like a long ways to the bottom. I weren't so sure I wanted to go down it, so I started to turn 'round to go back down the ladder part of the slide and that's when I seen the boys, Eddie and Beau.

"Hi!" I waved.

But they didn't say nothin'.

Then I seen they was carryin' an old dirty pillowcase.

"Whatcha got there?" I yelled.

They still didn't answer me, and it looked like they was goin' to the railroad tracks.

Then I thought I seen the pillowcase move, and I coulda swore I heared whinin' and a yelp.

"Daddy! I think Beau and Eddie got somethin' in that there sack. Wonder what they're up to?"

"Probably mischief," Daddy said as he lit another cigarette.

"Well let's go see," I said as I climbed back down the slide. When I got to the bottom, I took off runnin'.

"Timmy! Come back here; I have to go to work soon!" I heard Daddy holler.

I'M TIMMY

"Oh no!" I started to worry, "Maybe it's Sheba. Maybe they took her." I yelled back.

"Ah, they wouldn't do that," I heard Daddy say.

I ran as fast as I could, but the boys was faster. I tried runnin' on the rail of the railroad tracks, but I slipped and fell. That's when the train whistle blowed.

"Timothy Allen! Get off them tracks right now!" I heard Daddy yell as he came running after me.

I had to get down there and see what they got. I ran faster. This time, I tripped over one of those wooden railroad ties. I felt the sting on my legs and looked down to see little rocks and blood on my skinned knees.

The whistle blowed again. The train was gettin' closer.

"Timothy!" Daddy yelled. He sounded scared.

Then I heard him yell at the boys, "Hey! What are y'all doin'?"

I felt the ground shake. I bet they didn't hear him, 'cause the train was still comin' and it was real loud.

I seen Eddie throw that pillowcase on the ground and I could see Sheba's sweet eyes, only this time they looked scared. She was shakin' like she didn't know what was goin' on, and I didn't either.

I seen Beau lift her up by her back feet. Then Eddie took somethin' out of his back pocket and moved his arm real fast. Red watery stuff squirted out. Then, what looked like small balls fell to the ground. Beau took Sheba and threw her up on the railroad tracks just as the train rumbled by.

The boys yipped and yelled, laughin' as they each bent over and picked up what I thought was rocks from the ground. They started throwin' the rocks at the train. They weren't rocks. When the train passed me and daddy, I seen red splatters on the cars. I stood there, not bein' able to move until finally, I heard a scream that seemed to have been stuck in my throat.

Daddy ran over, scooped me up, and took off runnin'. Through my screams and tears, I could hear him in my ear saying, "It's okay, bubby, I got 'cha. Sick little bastards!"

"Why?" I screamed! "Why would they do such a thing? Oh, poor Sheba!"

Daddy didn't answer, but he ran carryin' me all the way home, and when we got back to our trailer, I was still cryin'.

Mama yelled from the bedroom, "what's he squawlin' 'bout?"

"Timmy just saw somethin' upsettin,' that's all."

"He ain't hurt, is he?" She grunted like an ole bear.

"No, no, he'll be alright."

I'M TIMMY

"Then tell him to shut the hell up; I'm tryin' to sleep."

"Here, bub, go to your room and try not to bother your mama, okay?"

I followed daddy to the bathroom. The door was closed part way, but I could still see him through the crack.

He splashed some water on his face, and I heard him say again, 'Damn, sick little bastards". He dried his face on the towel and reached for his clothes hangin' on back of the bathroom door.

"Daddy?" I sniffed, "Daddy do ya have to go to work today? Can't ya stay home just this once?"

Daddy turned and looked at me. He got down on his knee and looked me in the eye. He reached over and got a piece of toilet paper, and told me to blow my nose. I did.

Then, when he was wipin' my face, he said, "I hate to leave you, but I have to go to work. One day, you'll understand."

"But daddy, please, can't ya stay?" I begged.

"Please, bubby, don't make me feel any worse than I already do. Listen, tomorrow I'll do somethin' 'bout what them boys done." Daddy promised. "In the meantime, try not to think about it, okay? Now, I gotta go."

He kissed me on the top of my head and then went to his and mama's room. I heard him tell her goodbye before he ran out the door.

I went back to my room and crawled up on my bed. Daddy told me to try not to think about it, but that's all I could do. I didn't know what he was gonna do 'bout it tomorrow, but I knowed this... I hated those boys for what they done, and someday when I was bigger and stronger, I was gonna' make 'em pay. And that's a promise I plan to keep.

The next day, I got up early. I didn't sleep good 'cause I was havin' dreams 'bout Sheba. She kept runnin' away, and I was tryin' to find her. Just when I was 'bout to grab her, the train went by, it's whistle blastin' so loud I put my hands over my ears and sat straight up in bed. It took me a minute to figure out where I was. I looked 'round and was there in my bed, safe. Then I remembered that Sheba wasn't, and I started cryin' all over again. I wish she'd run away from Eddie and Beau or that I'd stopped 'em.

I'M TIMMY

Then I remembered that daddy promised he was gonna do somethin' 'bout what they done, so I ran to his room as fast as I could. Right as I was about to knock, mama whispered from the kitchen. "Timothy! What do you think your doin"?

I told her that I was gonna talk to daddy 'cause me and him had somethin' to do today.

"Don't you dare go in there, or I'll bust your ass. You're not gonna bother your daddy right now he's sleepin', so get back in your room and be quiet."

"But, Mama," I whined, 'this is real important."

"I don't care. You're not goin' in there. Now git back to your room 'fore I git my paddle!"

I went back to my room and waited for forever. Finally, I heard daddy coughin' and clearin' his throat in the bathroom. I ran to the bathroom door and knocked.

"Daddy? Ddddaddy, do you remember what you promised yesterday?

"I sure do, bubby. Let me get ready and we'll go."

"Go where?" I asked.

"To the police station."

I remember the clouds that day as we walked to the station. It almost seemed later than it was 'cause, they was so dark. I sniffed in a big breath and swore I could smell the rain comin'. That was one of my favorite smells. As we passed the church on the corner, I heard the bells ringin' lettin' all the people know it was time to go home. A whole bunch of people came out and walked down the steps.

"Looks like a storms comin'" A man said to his wife.

A big wind blew up her dress and she was holdin' her knees together as she smoothed it back down.

"Hurry, Hank, let's get home," the woman said.

Another big wind came and blowed the hat off his head. The man ran after it and it looked like him and that hat was racin' each other to the car. He grabbed it just before it went under the front tire. The man opened the car door and his wife scooted inside.

I took Daddy's hand. Church people dress a lot different than Daddy. The man runnin' to his car had on a tie and his shoes was mighty shiny. I could tell by the look in Daddy's eyes that he really liked the man's car.

We ain't got no car.

Sometimes, when we have to go to another town, like Jackson, Daddy takes us in his work truck. Mama always holds her head down and ducks behind the seat if she sees somebody she knows. Daddy looks real sad when she does that.

I like ridin' in the big truck. It smells like fresh cakes and pies that daddy takes 'round to all the neighborhoods and grocery stores. Sometimes, if he has any cakes left over, he brings 'em home to me.

But getting' back to goin' to the police station, all the way there, I was wishin' and hopin' that Eddie and Beau would be sent away and locked up forever.

When we got to the big red brick buildin', I let go of Daddy's hand and he helped me pull the heavy glass door open. I stood behind him as he walked up to the tall counter. I could barely see over the counter even standin' on my tippy-toes, but I heared someone typin' on a typewriter. It was a big man in a police uniform. He came up to the counter, looked at daddy, and said, "Can I help you?"

Daddy started tellin' him about the "Rogers" boys, he called 'em. The officer said he knowed who they was. I didn't want to think about what daddy was tellin' him. Instead, I started thinkin' bout how good it was gonna be with 'em gone.

Until I heard the man say, "Sorry, there's nothin' I can do about it."

Daddy said he thought that what they done was animal cruty and that was a mis, mis... somethin' I can't remember the word.

The officer told him in some states it was, but not here in Mississippi.

My eyes filled with tears when me and Daddy headed back out those big heavy doors.

"Don't cry, Timmy, I got another idea," he said as he took my hand and we headed back towards home.

I ran up on the porch when Daddy said, "Wait a minute, Tim, we ain't goin' home just yet."

"Where we goin'?"

"To talk to those boys, Daddy."

"Oh, no, I don't think that's a good idea," I said. I tugged on his arm to stop. "Oh! Please, Daddy, let's just go home."

"No, Timmy, somebody's gotta make them boys 'ccountable for what they done."

I was so worried I started bitin' my nails.

Daddy musta seen I was scared 'cause he said, "Hey, Timmy, watch this".

He jumped on a crack on the sidewalk and said, "Step on a crack and break your Mama's back."

I'M TIMMY

"Oh, no, Daddy! I could never say such a thing! Not even playin.'" I loved my mama. She was so beautiful. I could never wish anythin' bad to happen to her, and I sure wouldn't want it to be on 'ccount of me.

Daddy messed up the top of my hair and said, "Sorry, bubby. I was just tryin' to make you feel better by playin' a game. I know how crazy you are 'bout you're mama. I won't do it again."

Those three blocks seemed like the shortest blocks I ever walked 'cause 'fore I knowed it, we was there. Standin' at the gate of Eddie and Beau's house. I couldn't believe how messy their yard was. There was tires and old cars with the windas knocked out of the front and sides of 'em, sat up on big blocks. The grass was so tall, I couldn't see the walkway, and it pricked my legs as we walked through it. The steps to the porch looked loose and I was 'fraid we might fall through if we stepped on 'em. I looked at Daddy again. I'd stopped beggin' him to go back home 'bout a block ago.

He must have seen somthin' in my eyes 'cause he said, "It'll be alright, bubby. Come on."

We made our way up onto the front porch when Daddy banged on the door so loud I heard the front windas rattle.

"Who the hell is it?" I couldn't tell if that was Eddie or Beau talkin'.

It turned out to be Eddie, 'cause he opened the door 'fore we could answer.

He looked at us real hateful and said, "What do you want?"

"I wanna speak to your father," Daddy said.

"Well, he's bus…" Eddie started to say, but some big man came to the door and pushed him out of the way.

Wow! He looked just like Eddie 'ceptin he was bigger. He had that same pinched-looking face. His hair stuck out like a rooster's butt on one side, and his eyes was dark and glassy. He had his hand down his unbuttoned pants, and in his other hand, he was holdin' a beer. He smelled like beer. I know, 'cause he smelled the same way mama did when she and daddy would go out honky-tonkin'.

He waddled out on the porch and leaned up against' the dirty railin' and I was thinkin' fer sure it was gonna fall.

"Well?" He asked.

I started to rock, Daddy put his hand on my shoulder and stopped me.

I'm Timmy

"Mr. Rogers? My name's Allen, and this here's my boy, Timmy."

"So?"

"Well, the reason we come here is 'cause yesterday me and Timmy seen your boys do somethin' awful. They killed a dog and her pups."

"And?" Mr. Roger's took his hand out of his pants and caught hisself 'fore he fell.

"And," Daddy sounded like he was gettin' fed up. "I thought you might wanna talk to your boys 'bout how what they done was wrong."

"Who are you, the dog police?" Mr. Rogers said.

Eddie started laughing, and I could hear Beau laughin' through the now-open winda.

"For Chrissake, you come all the way over here to tell me about what my boys done to some ole bitch? Sides, boys will be boys, and what my boys do is none of your damn business."

Mr. Rogers let out a big belch that stunk to high heaven. I could tell he was gettin' mad 'cause he was real loud and his face was turnin' red. Daddy just took out a cigarette and calmly lit it.

"Well, I'm makin' it my business," said Daddy as he blew smoke in Mr. Rogers face. "I went to the police station and I told 'em what your boys done, you know it could be considered a mis, mis," (darn, I wish I could remember what that word was).

Anyways, daddy went on and told Mr. Rogers his boys could get in a lot of trouble.

Course, this made Mr. Rogers real mad. And I thought he was gonna hit daddy when he said, "How dare you come here and threaten' my boys!"

The thunder cracked so loud I almost jumped out of my skin.

Some woman came runnin' through the doorway and pushed past Mr. Rogers. She ran down the steps and started jerkin' her warsh off the line.

"Beau, Eddie, you boys git ouchere and hep me." She screamed.

Beau yelled through the open winda, "Awe, Ma, do we hafta?"

Then Mr. Rogers yelled, "course ya don't. How many times I told you, woman, my boys don't do women's work?"

"I didn't come here to fight," Daddy said as he blew smoke out of his nose and threw the end of his cigarette into the pourin' rain.

He grabbed my hand and took me back down the steps. The rain was comin' down so hard, it felt like little pebbles hittin' me all over. He grabbed a towel and threw it over me as he helped Mrs. Rogers' get the rest of her warsh down. "I just thought maybe you and me could talk this out man to man, but I see that ain't gonna happen," he yelled back up to Mr. Rogers.

"Git away from my wife, you sombitch! And don't you ever set foot here again. I'll beat you to a pulp."

He bent the beer can and he threw it at daddy, but the rain was fallin' so hard, it just fell to the ground.

Daddy took the towel off me and threw it in Ms. Rogers basket. We took off running ' cross the street and stood under the cover of a little store. Being Sunday, it was closed. I wanted to go ahead and run home, but Daddy said no, we would just wait it out.

Mr. Roger's, Eddie, and Beau stood on the front porch lookin' at us like they'd shoot us with their eyes if they could. Then Eddie put his hand to his mouth and yelled, "She- ba! She -ba! Oh, where could you be?" He and his brother thought that was the funniest thing.

Mr. Roger's must not of thought it was that funny though, 'cause he started smackin' Eddie in the head and yellin' "I told you, you little piece of shit, if you was ever gonna do somethin' like what ya'll done to that mutt, make sure nobody sees ya!"

As me and daddy stood there with the rain falling down, I asked him if he was gonna tell that lady what happened to Sheba. He asked me, "What do you think?"

I told him, "Well, from what I seen, I wouldn't want to know."

He said, "Alright then."

And that was the last time we ever talked about it.

And yeah, I guess that was it. That was how all the trouble with Eddie and Beau started. Ever since then, they've made me feel like I would want to be anybody but me. Always pickin', always hittin' and doin' anything they could to get me in trouble. But you know what? I never did tell Daddy. 'cause I rememberd what Mr. Roger's said and I didn't want to do anything that was gonna get my daddy hurt.

The bus jerked to a stop. Chester, the bus driver said he'd done told us three times to simmer down. But, I never heared him. Well, here he come stompin' up the aisle of the bus like a big ole bull. When he got up to us, I could smell the wintergreen tobacco in his mouth. I was shocked when he grabbed Eddie and Beau by the shirt collar at the same time. He yelled for them to get "their asses up to the front of the bus."

"Why us?" Eddie yelled back at him. "We ain't done nothin'."

But Chester said, "'cause I said so, now git!"

I'M TIMMY

Beau looked at me as he squeezed between the seats and said, "Boy, are you gonna git it!"

Eddie looked at me and put my comic book in his back pocket.

I yelled at him, "Gimme back my book!"

He turned around and tossed it way to the back of the bus.

"No!" I yelled when I thought it was gonna go out the opened winda. It didn't and I had to crawl down on that dirty bus floor to get it back.

Chester went back to the driver's seat. He spit out the winda 'fore he looked at all of us and said, "Now sit down and shut up!"

He sat there and stared at each of us for a long time through his mirror. I guess when he was sure we was gonna do as he said, he started the bus back up again.

I was glad to finally get to sit down. I scooted into the seat Eddie and Beau had been hidin' in and I put my comic book over my eyes. Boy, that wind was a blowin' in that winda like a hot furnace. It almost took my breath away.

I started thinking about daddy. For the past three days he'd been home when I got there. I didn't get to see him a lot 'cause he worked two jobs and was gone 'fore I got home. Then when he got home, it'd always be so late that I'd be already asleep.

But, like I said, not for the past three days. His big white snack truck would be sittin' in the driveway. He'd be in the back gettin' all of his trays ready for the next day. Man, my mouth would water just thinkin' bout all them cakes and pies. I liked to sneak up on Daddy and scare him. He'd be in the back there whistlin', and I'd sneak 'round and jump out shoutin' "Boo!"

He'd fall against the trays, first to one side and then the other. Then he'd grab his chest, and fall down and flop 'round like an old fish stranded on the riverbank. Finally, he'd stick his legs straight up in the air. He'd shake a little bit more 'til he stuck his tongue out and went quiet.

First, I'd think he was playin', and then he'd stay still for a long time. So I'd creep into the truck, and crawl up to his chest, and lay my head on it. I'd whisper, "Daddy?"

He'd just lay there. So, I'd get a little closer and get right up to his ear when he'd open his eyes and grab me and start ticklin' me. Sometimes, he tickled me so hard I got the hiccups, and other times I almost peed my pants.

I'd say, "Daddy! You scared me!"

He'd say, " Well, you scared me! What's the big idea sneakin' up on a feller like that?"

Then he'd tickle me some more, and we'd run 'round the truck 'til he'd be breathin' all hard and say, "Stop, stop, I need a truce."

"Can we play again, Daddy?" I'd always beg.

Most the time he'd tell me, "Sorry, bubby, I ain't got much time."

I'd ask him if he had to go that night and he'd say yes, and tell me to go warsh up for supper. Usually, I'd stand there and look into his green eyes and wait real quiet like. I couldn't tell if he'd really forgotten or was just pullin' my leg. Then he'd snap his fingers and say, "Oh! I pert ner forgot didn't I?"

He'd pull out a snack cake all wrapped in a paper sack, and say, "Is this what you was wantin'?"

I'd smile real big, and he'd make me promise not to eat it 'til after supper.

My daddy sure is swell.

I jumped when I felt somethin' hit me on top of my head. It was Billy Joe, tellin' me, "wake up, this here's your bus stop". I guess I must've fallen' 'sleep.

All the kids on the bus was actin' funny. Lookin' and pointin' at my trailer. Most of 'em had moved over to one side to get a better look. They was all talkin' and whisperin'.

There was a Mississippi State Police car sittin' right in front of my house. The red patrol lights was still flashin'. I could see the color blinkin' on the tin of our trailer. I put my comic in my back pocket and hurried down the aisle. Eddie stuck his monster of a foot out an' before I saw it, I tripped. I hit that metal floor hard, and when I got up, I could taste the salty blood in my mouth. Of course, everyone thought this was so funny. I thought, as the blood pooled under my tongue, how funny it'd be if I spit it out on Eddie. But when I looked at him, I knowed that'd be even more trouble, sos I just swallowed it instead.

"Better run along, " Eddie smirked. "Cops are probally here to throw your old man in the pokey."

'They ain't gonna do that." I told him.

"Hurry up, Kid," Chester told me. "I'm already runnin' late 'cause of you!"

I'M TIMMY

I jumped from the middle step, through the opened door to the ground. Chester pulled the door closed as the bus shuddered away.

Chapter 2

THAT STINKIN' BLACK smoke from the bus made me cough. I stared up at the officer standin' on my porch, then I looked round for Daddy's truck. It wasn't here, so they must not bet here to get him. I tried to figure out what they was doin, but I couldn't. Not even when I walked past the officer who was comin' down the steps as I was goin' up.

My Aunt Erma was standin' inside the door with another officer. "What are you doing here?" I asked her.

I'M TIMMY

"Well, it's about time! What took that bus so long?" she said.

I heard cryin 'comin' from my Mama's bedroom.

"Mama?" I panicked.

I went runnin' down the hall towards her door. She was sittin' on top of her bed. I could tell she'd been cryin' 'cause her eyes was all red. She put her hand out towards me, but when I got to the doorway, she slammed the door in my face.

"Mama!" I knocked on the door. "What's the matter? Can I please come in?"

Someone grabbed me. It was my Uncle Bob. "Here, Timmy, let's leave your Mama alone for now. Come on into the kitchen, me and you're Aunt Erma's got somethin' to tell ya. Erm? You gonna give me a hand here?" My Uncle asked.

"In a minute." My Aunt Erma smirked "Can't you see I'm talkin' to this police officer? Now, what was you sayin?"

"Well, I was sayin' your sister-in-law was alone when we first arrived to give her the news. We should have waited 'til someone else was here. At first, she seemed okay. Now that I think about it, she was probably in shock. It wasn't 'til after we left that we got a call from a neighbor about a disturbance here."

T. S. Kincaid

My Aunt Erma just stared at that man like he was the only one here. She was holdin' his hand from where he tried to shake hers, and she acted like she didn't want to let go. She was leanin' up against the door frame and rubbing her yellow hairdo, all done up like a bees nest on the top of her head, playin' with her side curls.

"When we returned," the officer went on, "she was goin' nuts! Throwing things, grabbing onto the curtains. I thought for sure she was tryin' to hang herself."

"Oh, my!" Erma said.

'Then," he kept sayin', "she went into the kitchen and grabbed that butcher knife. My partner grabbed her hand just before she cut herself. We tried our best to make her feel better."

"Oh, I'm sure you did," Erma told him. "I'm sorry it took so long to track us down. Officer... Rigby, is it?"

"Yes, but you can call me James." The Officer said.

"Okay...James," Aunt Erma smiled. "I'm sure the news is all over town by now. A town this size, you can't keep nothin' quiet. Gossip, gossip, gossip, that's all they do around here. Anyways, thanks again for waitin', I'm sure my sister-in-law will be fine."

"She was in such a state, I thought for sure we were gonna have to transfer her to the asy..."

I'M TIMMY

The officer looked over at me. I was still waitin' with Uncle Bob. Waitin' to be told what was going on. Waitin' to be able to talk, for I knew good and well, children should be seen and not heard.

"Erma! Are you comin'?" My Uncle Bob raised his voice.

"I said, in a minute!" she snapped back at him. Then she leaned over and whispered somethin' in Officer James Rigby's ear. The two smiled as she pushed the door open. He turned and looked at me one last time. It looked like he was gonna say somethin', but instead, he turned and walked away.

Aunt Erma looked over at Uncle Bob with a mean look on her face. She reached over to the coffee table and grabbed her pack of cigarettes. She started hittin' the pack on the palm of her hand. Then she opened the pack and had just finished lightin' one when a car pulled up in our driveway. Then another and another.

Smoke came out of her mouth when she said, "Oh, lord, Bob! Here they all come. We'll all be squeezed in this tin can like a girdle on a fat woman. I sure hope Lou Ann defrosted that ice box last week like she said she was gonna do. All that food they'll be bringin' is likely to spoil in this here heat."

"Hi!' Aunt Erma said, 'ya'll come on in."

T. S. Kincaid

There was all kinds of people walkin' 'cross our yard. All carryin' food, and sayin'" I know, isn't it terrible?" Or, " what a way to go."

I didn't know most of 'em. But some I did, like Miss Baxter, the playground monitor at my school. She came up to me and said, "Oh, Timmy, you poor little thing. I'm so sorry 'bout your daddy, honey."

I looked at her and said, "What 'bout Daddy?"

She gave Erma a dirty look and said, "Oh, Erma, you mean he don't know? Ain't you told him yet?"

Aunt Erma's face turned red and she said, "Well, we haven't had the chance to yet. We was just getting' ready to when ya'll pulled up."

"Well, for pity's sake," Miss Baxter said while shaking her head. "the boy needs to know."

She walked on into the kitchen and put what smelled like bescetti on the table.

Now, I had all kinds of questions. I looked round the room. I was lookin' for someone, anyone, but Aunt Erma or Uncle Bob. Then I saw him. My cousin Larry. His eyes saw mine and they got real big. He pointed for me to go outside. At first I acted like I didn't see him. But when I looked back, he was still starin' at me. This time he said with his lips, Go Outside!

I'M TIMMY

I shook my head no. He looked like he'd like to pound me, and I finally gave in. He went out the back door and met me 'round the corner of the trailer. We walked through the grass and went behind the old shed that was there when we moved here. Daddy liked to keep all of his yard tools in there.

Larry leaned up against it with one leg folded behind him and the other on the ground. To my surprise he reached in his pocket and pulled out a cigarette and put it between his lips.

"Hey! Where'd ya get that?" I was shocked. "You'd better not smoke that or you'll be in big trouble!"

He grabbed me by the front of my shirt and slung me around puttin' his heavy arm up against my chest. I couldn't breathe.

He got right up in my face and said, "Not if somebody keeps his big mouth shut, I won't. " The cigarette was moving up and down between his lips as he was talkin'.

You gotta know, Larry was a lot bigger than me. He had bright red curly hair that always looked like it needed a good brushin'. I was seven and a half, but he was bout' five or six years old when I was bornd, so he was a lot bigger. His whole body was covered in freckles. He even had three on his lips that I'd never noticed until now.

"I I I won't say nothin'." He was scaring me, and it was making my voice repeat my letters. I was gettin' better at talkin', but sometimes when I got real upset, my voice still did that. Mawmaw Pike called it stutterin'. She said she used to do it when she was little and so did my Mama. She said our brains was workin' faster than our mouths could talk.

"That's what I thought!" Larry said as he raised his arm off my chest.

I turned to run, but he caught me by the back of my shirt and said, "Wait a minute, I got somethin' to ask ya."

"What?" I took a deep breath.

"How does it feel? Larry asked.

"How's what feel?" I had no clue what he was talkin' bout.

"You know…" He moved his arm aroun' like he was wantin' me to spit somethin' out.

I looked at him and did the same thing. Then I flipped my hands over and shrugged my shoulders.

"Come on, damnit, quit actin' like you don't know what I'm talkin' bout!"

I'm Timmy

"I don't know what you're talkin' about. Look, I just wanna go. I'm tired of playin' this game." I finally said.

"Bein' half an orphan, stupid!" Larry blurted out.

"What's that mean?" I looked at him with my eyebrows squinted together. I did that when I didn't understand somethin'.

"You mean to tell me that you're so dumb that you ain't got it figured out yet?"

"Figured out what?" I was startin' to get mad now.

"Your daddy's dead, you idiot!"

I wasn't sure if I heard him right, so I said, "What are you sayin'?"

"Dead. D.E.A.D., you dummy! You know, as in bit the dust, bought the farm, dead as a doornail."

Man, did I get mad—madder than I ever was before. "You're a liar!" I screamed and pushed Larry back up against the shed.

"No, I'm not, you jerk!" Larry yelled, pushing me down to the ground. "Your daddy is graveyard dead, I'm tellin' you!"

I sat there frozen. His words really packed a wallop. All the sudden a big black cloud came round my head, and I couldn't see or hear nothin'. When I opened my eyes, I was layin'' on the ground lookin' up at the half moon, but it was still daylight. It all came rushing back to me what Larry said, and I knew I had to get away from him. I had to get to my Mama and find out what was really goin' on. Tears were in my eyes, and I was havin' a hard time seein'. I took off runnin' through the grass and bumped into a couple of cars that was parked everywhere. I finally got to the front door and into the trailer.

I bumped into a lot of people who said, "Hey! Watch it!"

I finally got through the crowd, and there was my Mama. Her door was opened now. A lot of people was standin' round her. She was sittin' on her bed like a queen. Even though I could tell she'd been cryin', I could still see her beautiful purpleish/blue eyes. They were the prettiest eyes I ever seen. Her hair was all done up on the top of her head. It was as black as the black bird I'd seen when livin' with Mawmaw Pike. Everyone said mama looked like that actress, Lisabeth? Oh, what was her name? It's right on the tip of my tongue. She played in that movie about a Giant.

"Mama?" I stood in the doorway, too scared to go in. " Mama?" I said again. "Pppplease tell me what Larry said ain't true. Please say this is all a joke and really, everyone is here for a big party."

I'm Timmy

"Party!" she screamed. "No, Timothy, this ain't no damn party. Jesus Christ! Git out of my sight, you little ass hole."

I barely had time to duck before she threw what looked like an ashtray at me. It hit the wall instead, and tiny pieces of glass went everywhere. I don't know what came over me, but I busted into tears, and alls I could hear were loud screams comin' from my own mouth. I threw myself on the floor and started kickin' and kept right on screamin'. Tiny pieces of glass got on my britches and shirt and it felt like I was bein' stabbed all over like a million times. Someone come and scooped me up. I thought it was daddy, cause he always done that when I was upset.

"Ddddaddy?"

But when I looked at him, it was Uncle Bob who had me. He carried me out into the backyard. He shook me and told me to be quiet. I didn't listen, I couldn't. I couldn't believe that my daddy was gone, and mama was actin' like a crazy person. What was wrong with her? Why didn't she hold me and tell me she loved me? I didn't make daddy go away. This was all too much. Before I knew it I was lying on the ground. My Uncle Bob had hit me. I mean, he really hit me. Like hard. I couldn't believe it. I stopped cryin' and looked at him with hurt in my eyes. My Uncle Bob had never hit me.

"I'm sorry, boy, but you've got to calm down." He finally told me.

I lay there. My body jerkin' each time I took a deep breath until I finally quit movin' at all. I was so tired. Uncle Bob picked me up and toted me back inside to my room. He laid me on the bed and left me there, closin' the door behind him. I was glad he brought me to my bed. I wanted to sleep, but all of the people comin' in and out of the house kept me awake for the longest time. It was so hot, so I kicked off my pants. The little pieces of glass scraped against my legs, scratchin' me and makin' 'em sting again. I tried flippin' my pillow over from one cool side to the other. This didn't help, not this time. This time, I had to keep wipin' the sweat off my head and face. My head started hurtin'. Even rockin' didn't help me this time.

I wanted daddy. I wanted all of these people to go away. I wanted everythin' to be like it was this mornin' when I woke up to the sound of daddy's truck runnin' outside my winda. And mama, what was she doin'?

I'M TIMMY

Didn't she love me anymore? Maybe she wishes it'd been me who died instead of daddy.

I thought about him and 'bout what Eddie and Beau would say 'bout all this.

Was daddy an angel now, watchin' over me an' mama? Daddy? Can you hear me? You an angel or are you a ghost? Do you walk around with a sheet over your head scarin' people? You remember, like I did last Halloween when you took me trick-or-treatin? Seemed like me and everyone else in the neighborhood was ghosts last year, 'Cept for Mary Jo. She was a witch. 'Member how mad mama got when you cut up her sheets to make me two eye holes? That thought kinda made me smile.

I tried to sleep, but my stomach growled. I was so hungry. We had all that food in there, and nobody brought me any of it to eat. Oh No! Now I had to go to the bathroom. I had to go so bad, but I couldn't. I couldn't take the chance of seein' somebody like Larry if I went out there. Or worse, mama. I can hold it, I told myself. Then I heard Miss Baxter talking to Aunt Erma at my door. I quickly shut my eyes. I heard the door squeak open, and my aunt say I was asleep.

T. S. Kincaid

She didn't try to be very quiet, 'cause if she was tryin' to whisper it weren't workin'. Miss Baxter asked her what exactly happened.

"Well, from what I heard," started Aunt Erma, in her half whisper, half mumblin' voice, "he had pulled over to change a tire on that old work truck of his. I guess the dumbass, I mean, the poor guy, thought he was over off the road far enough. He wasn't. ' Cause right about the time he got that tire off, along came one of them big tractor-trailer trucks, and bam!" Aunt Erma smacked her hands together, makin' me jump. I quickly rolled over. Erma didn't even lower her voice, "he was smashed flat as a pancake all over Interstate 55."

I covered my ears with my pillow. I didn't want to hear no more and had a hard time gettin' that picture outta my head. It reminded me of Sheba and how she had been squashed all over the railroad tracks.

"Oh my God, that's terrible!" said Miss Baxter. "Well, for pity's sake. You know these interstates are so dangerous."

"Oh, I know," said Aunt Erma. "Those trucks drive way too fast. They scare me to death. That driver said he didn't even see him if you can believe that."

Miss Baxter made a clicking noise by hittin' the back of her teeth with her tongue. I heard her make that noise 'fore and I'd tried to do that same sound a time or two.

She'd always click her teeth and shake her head at the same time, 'specially when I'd tell her the things that Eddie and Beau done.

I coughed and flipped over again.

Miss Baxter asked Aunt Erma what was to become of me and mama now.

Aunt Erma opened the door and they both sneaked out. I didn't get to hear what she said, and that left me worryin' and wonderin' the same thing.

Chapter 3

I JUMPED OUTTA bed as soon as I heard the bus wheels squeak. Oh No! My bed was wet. Now mama would give me a double beatin.' For missin' the bus and peein' the bed. I opened my door real slow. I didn't see nobody. They musta all gone home last night. I ran down the hall to the bathroom when all the sudden the door flung open and there was mama. Just standin' there. I froze. She came up to me and put her arms around me. She held me real tight and sniffed my hair.

Doin' all the things I wish she'd done the night b'fore. I still didn't move.

She pushed me away and said, "What's your problem?"

"Nnnnothin'" I said. I just stood there lookin' at her, wonderin' if I should tell her 'bout my sheets or not. Surely she knowed I missed the bus. It looked real bright outside and I could tell it was past time to get up.

"Mmmmama"

"Quit that damn stammerin,'" She said, "You sound like an idiot!"

"Yyes'm," I said. I took a deep breath an' tried to think real hard 'bout what I wanted to say. "Mama, I'm sorry I missed the bus." Hey! I got it out.

I quickly put my arm up, waitin' for her wallop.

But guess what?

Mama didn't hit me. She didn't seem mad at all. She just said, "Awe that. Well, I don't think you'll be goin' back to school, least 'till Monday. Then she put her hand under my chin, kissed me on my forehead and said, "Go find your Aunt Erma, and tell her to fix ya somethin' to eat."

Mama walked back into her room, like nothin' she did yesterday ever even happened. But that was mama. Sometimes she ran hot and sometimes she ran cold as daddy'd say. I sure am glad she's feelin' better. There was times when we didn't know what mama would do. Most times me an daddy just stayed real quiet and tried to stay out of her way when she was in one of her moods.

I was in my room when I heard her singin' in the shower. Later, she came out of her room all dressed up in one of her best dresses. She looked so pretty. Taylor, that was it. Most people said she looked just like Lizabeth Taylor. I knowed I'd think of it.

Mama said to stay with Aunt Erma while she and Uncle Bob went and took care of some things. I don't know why they didn't go in Uncle Bob's car. Maybe 'cause Aunt Erma needed it later. Anyways, I seen 'em walkin' towards the bus stop.

When I finished eatin' I went back to my room. I was tryin' to decide what to do about my sheets when Aunt Erma came in.

"Now, I told your Mama that I was only gonna stay here 'til your Grandma Pike got chere." Aunt Erma said.

"Mawmaw Pike's comin'? Yippee!" I hollered.

"Yes," she griped. "that old biddy better get here soon, too."

I didn't know what an old biddy was, but it didn't sound very nice.

"Well, boy, I guess it's up to me to see if you got anything decent to wear to the funeral. Let's look in your closet."

She pulled the curtain back that was hangin' in place of a door.

"Ha! Just what I thought! You ain't got nothin'. I guess your mama 'spects me and Uncle Bob to foot the bill for you some new clothes, huh?."

"Yes, Ma'am!" I was excited to think I was gonna get new clothes.

"Well, if that's what your mama thinks, she's got another thing comin'." She had her mean face on.

"If she thinks me and your Uncle are gonna spend our hard-earned dollars on you, that ain't happenin'. We ain't got no magic money tree growin' out in the grove, ya' know?"

She kept on talkin' 'fore I could answer.

"No, I'll just have to look up in the attic when I get home and see if there's any of Larry's old clothes still around. Lord knows Larry might have somethin'. Although I don't think he was ever as puny as you. You an' your daddy's people must've all been runts. I always felt sorry for your mama getting' stuck with that good for nothin' daddy of yours."

I could feel my face getting' real hot.

"She sure was a looker, still is. I guess that's why your daddy had to get her drunk sos he could take advantage of her. There's no way she woulda done it with that troll on purpose. Only reason she gave in and married the asshole is 'cause she got knocked up with you. I'd have taken my chances with the coat hanger if it'd been me."

I didn't get most of what she was sayin' but I knowed none of it was nice about daddy. I got so mad 'fore I knowed it the words, " Don't you talk about my Daddy like that! My Daddy's a good man, better than you or anybody else…" ran straight out my mouth.

I felt a sting across my face. I hunkered down when I saw her raise her hand to slap me again.

"How dare you talk to me like that! I oughta bust your ass right here and now!" she yelled.

Her hand was still raised when we heard a car pull up in the driveway.

I took off as fast as I could to the winda. It was Mawmaw Pike. I raised my hand to bang on the winda and wave when I felt myself bein' pulled away and I was slidin' across the floor.

"Oh, no you don't" Aunt Erma slung me so hard I skidded across the floor and ended up hittin' the wall of my room. She slammed the door.

"You stay in there 'til I say so, you got that? That'll teach you to talk to me like that. One word outta you, and I'll get one of your daddy's belts." She promised.

I ran to the door as soon as I heard her walk away. It was locked. I threw myself on my pee-soaked sheets, beatin' my mattress with my fist. I went back to the door and put my ear against it. I heard her open the outside door for Mawmaw Pike. Boy, she sure could turn her voice from mean to nice real fast.

"Why, Mother Pike," she sounded so sweet," I didn't hear you out there. Come on in the kitchen, I got a nice fresh pot of coffee waitin' for ya."

"How's Timmy?" My Mawmaw asked.

"Oh, he's just fine, naturally he's upset about his daddy and all".

Mawmaw must have asked about me again, 'cause I heard Erma tellin' her "No, really he's fine. He just needs to rest is all. Now come on and get that cup of coffee, I insist. You wouldn't want it to go to waste now would ya?"

Thank goodness Mawmaw wasn't buyin' all her jibber jabber. She came straight to my door and tried to turn the handle. Then she knocked. "Timmy, you in there?"

"Yes, Mawmaw!" I yelled.

"Well, what's the door doin' locked?"

"Aunt Erma locked me in!"

"I did no such thing!" Erma lied.

"What on earth? " I heard Mawmaw jiggle the handle and unlock the door.

"Mawmaw!" I yelled as I ran to her and jumped into her arms.

"My Tiny Tim!" She said, sliding me over onto her hip. "Although you ain't so tiny no more are ya."

She put me down. "Oh! Let me get a good look at you! My goodness, how you've grown."

"Mawmaw, I'm so glad you're here."

We heard a horn beep. The taxi was still outside.

"You ain't leavin' are ya?" I asked.

"No, honey, I just have to pay the man is all." Mawmaw explained.

"Well, don't look at me," said my aunt. " I'm not payin' him."

I'm Timmy

"I don't expect you to, I have to get the money from my suitcase, and I didn't want to open it in front of God and everybody," Mawmaw said.

She got out the cash and handed it to me.

"Here Timmy, go pay the man honey, and tell him to keep the change."

The cab driver seemed happy. When I ran back to the trailer, Aunt Erma and mawmaw was in the kitchen. Aunt Erma was tellin' her that mama and Uncle Bob went to town to take care of the 'rangements.

Aunt Erma was pourin' the coffee when I walked in. She glared at me real quick then she said, "Isn't it just awful? Poor thing was so upset last night. Too bad you couldn't be here when she really needed you."

"Well, I came as quick as I could. I rode here on the Greyhound bus all night, ya know."

"Of course you did, dear. I'm just sayin' that I'm glad that me and Bob were the ones here for her when it really mattered. Boy, she sure was in a state last night. Well, you of all people know how her moods can be. Screamin' like a banshee one minute and laughin' like a crazy person the next. Maybe it's best you weren't here. It took all we could do to calm her down. Even had to call the doctor to come give her a sedative. Tell me dear, does hysteria run in your family?'

Whatever Aunt Erma was sayin' was really makin' mawmaw mad. Aunt Erma was just sitting there pretty as you please, with that smug look on her face and sippin' her coffee, like they was talkin' 'bout the weather or somethin'.

But I could tell. When mawmaw gets mad she starts breathin' real hard, and her voice goes all high and squeaky.

"No more than anyone else's!" Mawmaw snapped.

"Well, you must be tired after your long trip, dear. You seem a little cranky. I would stay and give you a hand, but I've been here all night and I've got to get my rest too. You understand, I'm sure. I'll be goin' now. There's plenty of food in the icebox if you get hungry."

Erma stood up, her keys gingled as she grabbed her pocket book. "I'm sure Bob and Lou Ann will be back pretty soon. Least they better be. Larry stayed the night with a friend whose papa drove all the way over from Clinton. I need to get and see how he's doing. He's got a big game tonight."

Mawmaw Pike looked shocked. "Surely you're not thinkin' of goin' to a ballgame tonight after everythin' that's happened."

"Well, of course I am. Just 'cause somebody died don't mean we all have to stop livin'. Besides, it's important to Larry that we're there. Neither me, nor his father are gonna let him down."

"Don't you think it's important to Lou Ann for her brother to be here at a time like this?"

Mawmaw stood and put her arms on her hips. Her breathin' was real heavy.

I was wonderin' how long Aunt Erma could keep up her actin' 'cause 'bout that time she looked like she was gonna blow.

"Well, he has been! He's with her right now! What more do you people want? We have already taken time off workin' to be here, which is more than I can say for some people."

"Watch it now!" Mawmaw cut in.

"Look, I ain't gonna stand here and defend myself to you or anyone else 'bout what I do. Just 'cause Bob is Lou Ann's brother don't make him her keeper. Now we have done all were gonna do, and that's it. You got that?"

I stood there wide-eyed, with my mouth open. I ain't never heard nobody speak to my mawmaw like that. Mawmaw leaned over and put her finger in Aunt Erma's face.

"Don't you dare ever speak to me like that again! I may be older than you, but I can still whoop your ass.

Now I suggest you get outta here 'fore I really lose my temper. And let me tell you somethin' else. If you *ever* lay another hand on this child or lock him in a room again, we may be havin' to plan two funerals instead of one. You got that?"

"Oh!" Aunt Erma stomped her foot and took off through the house to the front door. She stopped and started to turn around until Mawmaw told her, "Good-bye, Dear'"

Aunt Erma stormed out on the front porch, stomped down the stairs, got into her car, and slammed the door. The tires squealed as she backed up and ran over mama's trash cans. I hear'd her say a cuss word or two as she was tryin' to put it in gear. They was really grindin'. She finally got it a goin' and took off so fast that all that was left was a trail of dust and gravel.

Me and Mawmaw stood at the winda lookin' at all the trash blowin' all over the yard.

"Bitch," said Mawmaw, "Good riddance!"

"When do you think she'll be back?" I asked.

"Oh, don't worry, Timmy, she won't be back as long as I'm here."

'But she's gotta come back." My eyes started waterin' again.

"Why, child, what's the matter?" She took my face in her hands and looked deep into my sad eyes. For the first time, I saw my mama's eyes in hers. Mama's eyes didn't have wrinkles around 'em like mawmaw's, but they was the same.

"She promised to bring me some of Larry's old clothes sos I could look nice for my daddy."

"Is that what she told you?" Mawmaw took a real deep breath.

"Well, don't you worry, honey. We'll get you somethin' real nice to wear for your Daddy. You don't have to wear Larry's old hand me downs.'

She took a tissue out of her pocket and wiped my eyes.

"Hey, I'm hungry, she said, "How 'bout you?"

"Yes ma'am." I said, "Miss Baxter brought some bescetti, would you like some of that?"

"You mean Spa-ghet-ti? Oh, I would love some."

We walked back into the kitchen and had just finished eatin' when we heard a car pull up.

'You don't think she's back again, do ya?" I asked.

I was worried there'd be another fight. I ran to the winda. This time it was another cab and I saw mama get out of it. Mawmaw came over and opened the door.

Uncle Bob threw up his hand and said, "Hi, Momma! I would stay, but I gotta go."

"Oh, I know, Erma told me all about it. You go on and I'll see ya later."

Mama came up on the porch. She had on big black sunglasses, and I couldn't see her eyes. She came through the door and said, "Hi, Momma, thanks for comin.'"

That was all she said. She walked straight on through the house, went to her bedroom, and closed the door.

'What 's wrong with her?" I asked.

"Nothin', honey, she's just havin' a hard time right now is all. We just need to leave her alone and let her get some sleep. Hey, you got any cards?"

I thought about it for a minute. "I don't think so," I sadly said.

"Well, go get my pocket-book. I think I got some. Ya wanna play?"

"Sure," I said as I ran to get her handbag.

Mama stayed in her room for the rest of the day, while me and mawmaw played Fish, Old Maid, and Crazy Eights. Mawmaw even washed my sheets and said that would be our little secret.

I'M TIMMY

Along evenin' time people started comin' round again. They didn't bring anymore food, but boy did they help themselves to what was brought the night before. Some of 'em brought beer, and this time it did seem more like a party. Lots of people were a lot louder than last night, too. Mama even came out of her room and turned on some music on the radio.

Mawmaw Pike came and crawled in bed with me. We squeezed in tight. She said she was tired and didn't feel like sittin' up with all of those hooli…, hooli, some other word I can't 'member.

I was so glad she was with me. She sure could snore loud, but I didn't mind. Anythin' was better than the night I'd had the night b'fore.

I had lotsa different feelin's. I was sad 'cause of daddy. But in a funny way, I was happy too. I mean, I didn't have to go to school and put up with Eddie and Beau, my Mawmaw Pike was here, and me and her was gonna go shoppin'. I hardly ever got to go to town. I finally fell asleep thinkin' about all there was to do tomorrow. I bet if I played my cards right, I just might get me an ice cream.

Chapter 4

"TIMMY," I HEARD my Mawmaw say, "Mr. Robin is callin' for you to wake up."

"Hummm?" I rolled over, yawned, and stretched.

"Come on, sleepyhead, says Mr. Robin."

I'M TIMMY

I listened again, and jumped out of bed and looked out my winda. That's right, now I remember, that was the sound of the robin.

"Come on, now. It's time to rise and shine. Your breakfast is waitin' on ya."

I took a big whiff and could smell the best smell in the world; my Mawmaw's delicious pancakes. She made 'em just my size, too. They was so crispy 'round the edges and light and fluffy in the middle. They was my favorite.

"Thank you, Mawmaw," I said when the last one was gone.

"You're welcome, child. Now hurry and get ready, we don't wanna miss the bus to Jackson. "

I ran and got dressed as fast as I could. I asked mawmaw if mama was comin', but she said not today. Today was gonna be our day.

We didn't have to wait long at the city bus stop 'fore it came rollin' down the street. We got on, but it was so crowded with all of the people goin' to town, that mawmaw had me sit on her lap, 'til it cleared out. I scooted over to the winda and watched all the cars and people go by. I loved going to the big city. It was so busy and loud. I could hear people beepin' their horns and men whistlin' at ladies.

We got to Kennsington's right before 11:00. Mawmaw said that was perfect, cause' that gave us an hour to shop 'fore lunch. She said if I was real good we would go to Pat's Pop Palace for a bite to eat 'fore headin' home. You better believe I was gonna be good.

I thought we'd look 'round the store, but mawmaw had other ideas. We went straight upstairs to the children's department. We looked 'round but didn't see anythin' she liked.   Finally, on a rack that said CLEARANCE, she found the perfect suit for me. Well, it wasn't exactly perfect 'cause when I tried it on she said, "Well, how's that feel?"

"It's a little tight," I said.

She tugged on my sleeves and made me raise my arms.

"Well, it is a little bit tight, but it will do in a pinch, and this certainly is a pinch."

I thought she was talkin' to me, but she sort of said it low, like she was talkin' to herself.

"Can we get a tie, too?" I asked.

I'M TIMMY

She looked at me and said, "We'll see. You still need a shirt and some shoes."

Then I felt bad for askin' 'cause the blue pants and matchin' jacket was more than enough.

"Okie dokie," I said.

We looked 'round some more and finally found a nice pair of shiny shoes. Just like the ones the man comin' out of the church had on. They were a little big, but Mawmaw said I could just wear some thick socks, and if I had to I could stuff some toilet tissue in the toes to make 'em fit better.

My stomach growled. Those little pancakes didn't stick to my ribs for very long.

"You ready to go get a bite to eat?" Mawmaw asked.

"Sure," I said.

We walked around the corner to Pat's and the door jingled when we opened it. Man, was it busy. People everywhere. The waitress and bus boys was runnin' 'round workin' as fast as they could to get a table ready. The place smelled like greasy french fries and smoke. The man in the window that led to the kitchen kept dingin' that litte bell and hollerin' "Pick up" faster than that waitress could keep up.

T. S. Kincaid

Mawmaw looked at the clock and said, "Oh, dear, I didn't think about it bein' lunch-time for everybody"

We waited at the door 'til a booth opened. Man, I gotta tell ya, that was the best tastin' hotdog I ever eat. They actually toasted their buns on the outside. They was so good. When I asked for another one, Mawmaw said why don't I save some room for dessert.

She was right. I really did want dessert. I ended up gettin' a rootbeer float. Two of my favorite things, rootbeer *and* ice cream.

By the time we got back home, I was tuckered out. I think Mawmaw was too, 'cause she said she was gonna go in my room and lay down for a little while.

People were still comin' over. Some brought more food and others brought more drink. There was not as many as there was the first night. Aunt Erma an' Larry came back over, but she stayed clear of mawmaw. It was funny watchin' her be so quiet. Larry kept tryin' to talk to me, but I acted like he weren't there. He finally left me alone. Mawmaw was still mad at him for the way he'd told me 'bout daddy.

See, Aunt Erma had had Larry 'fore she met my Uncle Bob. 'Course, everyone said it didn't make no difference, but Mawmaw always seemed mad about somethin' when it came to that. Even I noticed she treated Larry differen't from me. I think I was always her special one, and she was mine.

Mawmaw, mama, and Uncle Bob stayed up late into the night talkin' in the kitchen. The only thing I heard was mama sayin' "I don't know, I'll have to think about it."

The next day, mama was in one of her moods again. She kept sayin', "I'm a nervous wreck."

Mawmaw kept tellin' her to calm down and take one of her nerve pills. But mama didn't listen.

I put on my new suit, but really wished I could take it off as soon as I did. It was so hot and itchy. I kept tuggin' at it tryin' to stretch it out.

When I walked by the bathroom, mama grabbed my arm and jerked me in with her.

"Stop that fidgetin'. Now you listen to me, Timothy, this is gonna be a really hard day for me and I don't want you messin' it up. You better sit still and be on your best behavior, you hear me?"

She was taking the comb and raking it through my hair so hard that it was causin' it to hurt. I kept wincin,' but the more I did, the harder she raked. She took out some hair cream and tried to rub it into my hair. I guess that didn't work 'cause she threw the comb in the sink.

"Damn, you and that stupid cowlick of yours!" she screamed. "Get out of my sight!"

I ran from the bathroom in tears to my Mawmaw, who was sittin' out on the porch.

"My goodness, how handsome you look. Your daddy sure would be proud if he could see you now." She said.

"I want to see my daddy!" I cried.

"I'm afraid that ain't possible, honey. Listen, Timmy, look at me. It's best to remember your daddy the way he looked the last time you saw him.

About that time, Aunt Erma and Uncle Bob drove up.

"Ya'll ready?" asked Uncle Bob.

"Give me just a minute to get Lou Ann, we'll be right there." Mawmaw told him.

We all piled into the car with mama, Uncle Bob and Aunt Erma ridin' in front, and me, mawmaw, and Larry in back. At first, Larry threw a fit 'cause he wanted to ride up front, but mawmaw told him to "show some respect."

After a while, he gave in and slammed the door but pouted all the way to the church. It was a long hot ride. Both Aunt Erma and Uncle Bob was smokin' and even though they had the windas cracked, it was still makin' me carsick. I asked if we could roll the windas down some more, but Aunt Erma said no 'cause she didn't want to mess up her hair.

When we got to the church, there was all kinds of people there. I didn't know most of 'em. Miss Baxter came over and patted me on my sore head and asked me how I was doin'. I saw a couple of kids with their parents from my school, but that was 'cause their parents were good customers of daddy's.

I looked 'round for Eddie and Beau, hopin' they weren't there. They wasn't and I sure was glad.

I ain't never been to church. That's just somethin' we didn't do. When I walked in, I was amazed at the long wooden seats and the beautiful pictures on the windas. I ain't never seen nothin' like it

Mawmaw took my hand and led me to the second bench from the front. I scooted back as best I could on the slippery wood, but my legs dangled over the edge. My shoes, that was too big, kept slippin' off and goin' underneath the seat in front of me. I couldn't find any thicker socks and that toilet tissue didn't work.

Mama walked with Uncle Bob, behind me. She was all dressed in black and she had on a hat with a long black thing hangin' down in front of her face. How can she see? She was cryin' somethin' awful. I kept wonderin' if she was gonna grab that cloth hangin' down in front of her face and blow her nose with it. She kept getting' louder and louder and I thought for a minute they was gonna kick us out of there.

Aunt Erma was sittin' on the other side of Uncle Bob. Larry was sittin' beside her. I guess he got to sit up front after all. Anyways, I saw Aunt Erma roll her eyes and she leaned over to Larry and said, "Boy, she sure is playin' it to the hilt."

Mawmaw Pike reached over and smacked Aunt Erma on the arm warnin' her to be quiet.

"Ouch!" yelled Aunt Erma. She rubbed her red shoulder and looked over at mawmaw, she looked like she was bustin' to say somethin' but kept her mouth shut.

I didn't see any of daddy's people. Like me, he was an only child and he told me he growed up without a mama or daddy. They had died a long time ago. I guess I never thought about 'em 'til now.

We sat there in that hot church and I thought it was never gonna end. We stood up and sang songs while somebody played the piano, then we sat back down and was told to bow our heads and close our eyes.

All the ladies kept waving their fans 'round and I was wishin' I had me one. Then we would stand up and sing again. Then some man, I guess it was the preacher, stood up in the front and said a lot of nice things about daddy. I tried my best to sit still. My clothes was so itchy I just wanted to take 'em off.

Larry kept turnin' around and makin' funny faces at me. I tried not to laugh, but I couldn't help it a time or two. Then people would look at me with their eyebrows close together and whisper how disrespectful I was.

Larry turned around once more after I had settled down and Mawmaw Pike grabbed him by the arm and dared him to turn around again. She moved me over to the other side of her and told me to be still. Larry didn't turn around no more.

Finally, it was time to go back outside. We all had to go behind the church to the graveyard. Daddy's box was put in the ground. Mawmaw told me to take a clump of dirt and throw it on top of his box. I looked down in there and started to cry. Was daddy *really* in there? I hadn't seen him. I still kept thinking that maybe this was all a big joke and that daddy was gonna jump out and say, "Boo!" Just like I used to do to him. I waited for a while, but I guess not. 'Cause he never did.

We got back to the house and all of us ate again. Then Mawmaw said it was time for her to go. I cried and begged her to stay, but she said she had to get back home to her chickens and make sure her neighbor, Miss Margaret, who she helped look after, was doin' okay.

"I love you, Timmy, and I want you to know you're a good boy, you hear? Take care of your mama." Mawmaw said.

Uncle Bob drove her to the Greyhound bus station. I wanted to go with her, but was told no.

When he came back to get Aunt Erma and Larry, Mama ran into her room and slammed the door. She started screamin' and I could hear things smashin' up against the walls. Uncle Bob tried to talk to her. When he opened her door I could see she was tearin' up all daddy's photos. I didn't want her to do that and I wanted to yell for her to stop, but I didn't want her to take her anger out on me.

Mama finally settled down.

After everyone left, It was real quiet. It seemed funny all of the life that had been here before was now gone. It was almost like the house had died too.

In the middle of the night, Mama came to my bed. She ran her fingers over my sore head and snuggled up real close.

I'M TIMMY

She whispered in my ear, " I don't know what to do." I could tell she was cryin' 'cause my cheeks got all wet.

I rolled over and said, "Don't worry Mama,' as I wiped her tears away. "I'll take care of you."

Her voice changed, and she stiffened her body and said, "You silly little fool. Now you're nothin' but a walkin' liability."

Whatever that was.

Chapter 5

"TIMOTHY! YOU GET your ass out to that bus and don't you dare be late!" Mama screamed from her bedroom.

I shoved the burnt piece of toast I'd been eatin' between my teeth, and hopped across the yard with one shoe on and one shoe off. I stepped on the wet grass and got my sock all wet. I hated when that happened. I put my shoe on and it made a squishing sound as I walked.

I'M TIMMY

Now, my foots gonna be cold and wet for the rest of the day.

I finished the last bite of toast just as the school bus rolled up. I swallowed hard and took a deep breath. I saw Eddie and Beau right away, and I looked for the first empty seat I could find.

"Hey, Timmy," Eddie yelled.

I turned around and he waved, "Come here. We got somethin' for ya." He held up a little box and smiled.

I thought about it for a minute. There would probably be more trouble if I didn't go back there than if I did. I waited for the next time the bus stopped before I made my way back to where they was sittin'.

Eddie got up and said. "Here old buddy, you can sit with us."

I squeezed in between him and Beau. Beau put his arm around me and whispered in my ear, "Here's a little somethin' to remind you of your daddy."

"Thanks," I said. It made me feel good, they being so nice to me and all, I kinda smiled.

"Oh, don't mention it." Grinned Eddie. "it's just a little somethin' we scraped up for ya."

I took off the lid and carefully pulled apart the white tissue paper. My smile went away and my eyebrows squeezed together. You know like when I didn't understand somethin'?

Then it hit me all at once. Inside that wrapped tissue was a dead frog. It was all dried out and flat as the lid I had opened. It's guts had oozed out the sides and turned into sticky bubbles. It had one eye lookin' straight at me givin' me a creepy feelin'.

I screamed and threw it into the air. It landed on Mary Jo, who screamed too. Then she threw it. Before I knowed it, it was hoppin' round the bus as if it was alive again with all the people throwin' it all over the place.

Beau and Eddie busted out laughin'. I tried my best to get away, but I was in between them like a piece of cheese between two pieces of bread. The more I tried to get out, the tighter they squeezed. I finally put my hands over my ears to keep from hearin' 'em and cried all the way to school.

When they finally let me up, I ran as fast as I could to get out of the bus. Chester stopped me and said, "Boy, how come every time you get on this bus there's trouble? Am I gonna have to kick you off?"

I didn't know what to say, so I just turned and stumbled down the steps. I turned my ankle hard. I just wanted to sit there and cry, but finally, Miss Baxter saw me and came runnin' over. I tried to tell her what happened, but I couldn't get my words out. She helped me get up and into the school. Then helped me get to my classroom. But things there was just as bad.

All day long, people kept whisperin' and pointin' at me sayin', "there's the kid whose daddy just died," or "Yeah, did you hear about how his Mama was actin' at the funeral?" or some other things I didn't want to hear.

The day was terrible. I hated it. I wanted to go home, but knowed that I couldn't. I didn't have no way to get there. dMama couldn't come and get me and I didn't want Aunt Erma to. Alls I had to look forward to was waitin' to get back on that bus when the time came, and seein' and being scared of what them boys was gonna do next.

I was shocked when I got on the bus that afternoon. Chester had me sit in the seat right behind him. He said that would be my spot from now on. Eddie and Beau didn't look too happy about that, but I didn't care. I was just glad to be away from 'em.

Turns out the bus ride to and from school was the best part of the rest of that week. I tried to go to school each day and pretend that nothin' had happened to daddy. I thought maybe everybody would quit talkin' 'bout it so much. But they didn't. By the time I got home each day, I was so wore out from all that pretendin' that soon as supper was over I fell asleep.

I missed daddy.

Sometimes at night I'd talk to him.

I'd say, "Daddy? Are you there? If you are please talk to me." I guess he wasn't, 'cause he never did. Other nights I could hear mama in her room cryin' and listenin' to the radio.

Time went by and me and Mama went on. Once in a while, on weekends when I'd be out in the yard playin,' Beau and Eddie'd ride by on their bikes and yell, "She-ba." I could hear 'em laughin' all the way back down the street.

I got to where I didn't want to go out an play at all. That would always make mama real mad.

She'd say, "Go on outside, you're gettin' on my nerves. I can't stand you bein' underfoot all the time."

It felt like I didn't have no place to go. I sure was lonely. Boy, what I wouldn't do for one of them cakes Daddy used to give me right about now.

Chapter 6

I WILL NEVER forget, I come home one day and there was this girl sittin' in the livin' room. She had on a pretty pink skirt and her hair was up in a ponytail. I'm guessin' she was in high school, 'cause she had a stack of books sittin' beside her.

"Hi, I'm Timmy," I said.

"Hey," she said. She was chewing gum and blew one of the biggest bubbles I ever seen.

Mama was in the back bedroom gettin' ready to go out. I could tell cause I could smell her goin' out perfume. I walked back into her room and stood at her doorway. Sure enough, she was in one of her best dresses. The blue one that me and daddy liked. She had her hair all done up, like I liked it too. I just stood there watchin' as she put her lipstick on.

She jumped when she saw me through the mirror.

"Oh! Timothy! How many times have I told you not to sneak up on me like that?"

"Sorry, Mama, where you goin'?" I asked

"I'm goin' out for a little while."

"Can I go?" I looked at her with hopeful eyes.

"No!' She said in her 'I mean it' voice. "You stay here with Sally!"

"Who's that?" I asked.

"What are you blind, stupid? She's the girl sittin' in the livin' room. She's gonna be your babysitter tonight."

"How long will you be gone?"

"As long as I like, not stop askin' all these dumb questions." Mama huffed.

I'M TIMMY

Sally came to Mama's door. "Excuse me," She said. "I have to be home by 10:00 tonight. It's a school night ya know?"

Sally blew another bubble. This time it was so big it popped all over her pimpled face. She pulled the sticky goo off with her fingers and put it back in her mouth.

Mama told her, " sure no problem."

She finished getting' ready when I heard a horn blow from the front yard.

I ran to see who it was, but Mama told me to get to the kitchen and get my dinner.

"But, I want to see who it is." I told her.

"Never you mind, you nosey thing. Now get in that kitchen and do as I say."

She went out the front door. I guess she forgot to tell me good-bye.

After I ate my macaroni and cheese, I asked Sally if she wanted to play some cards. Mawmaw Pike left hers here.

She said no and that she had some studyin' to do cause she had a big test tomorrow. I finally just went in my room tried to stack all those cards together and make a house out of 'em. They kept fallin', but I kept tryin' 'til I got tired and crawled into bed.

T. S. Kincaid

I woke up to someone hollerin'. I knowed it was late cause it was still dark and the moon was shining through my winda on my pillow. That didn't happen 'til way up in the early mornin'.

"Look, Lou Ann, I told you I had to be home by 10. Now I'm in big trouble 'cause my Pop is gonna be really mad at me." Yelled Sally.

"Oh, I'll talk to your Poppa, honey, I'm sure he'll understand." Mama was talkin' kinda funny. Like she did when her and daddy would come home after they'd been out.

"Did your ride leave? How am I gonna get home now?" I could tell Sally was real upset.

I didn't want her and Mama to fight, so I sneaked out of my room and peeked my head in to see what was goin' on.

"Walk, like I do." Said Mama.

"Are you kiddin' me? It's almost 2 o'clock in the mornin'!" Shouted Sally.

"Oh, hell! Ain't nobody gonna eat ya." Mama said.

'Just give me my money, so I can go." Sally said.

"Well, you see honey," Mama put her hand up and squeezed her finger and thumb together and made 'em real small. She squinted one eye. "There's just a lil' ole problem with that." She pouted her lips and shook her head. "I ain't got none."

"What!? Look Lou Ann I want my money." Demanded Sally.

"Well," said Mama, " You can't squeeze blood outta a rhubarb." Then she sort laughed.

"You're really some piece of work!" Sally yelled as she slammed the door. "Nobody, babysit for Lou Ann," She hollered "She'll stiff ya!"

"Kiss my ass!" Mama screamed as she slammed the door. She banged against the wall a few times as she zigzagged down the hall to her room. I followed her. She flopped down on her bed.

"Mama, did you have a good time tonight?" I asked as I was takin' off her shoes. She answered me with a deep breath and a snore. I put the covers over her and kissed her goodnight.

I went back through the trailer. After I locked the door, I thought about turnin' out the lights, but I was too 'fraid of the dark, so I left 'em on.

Mama seemed to go out a lot. There was always someone new sittin' in the livin' room when I'd come home from school. Seems like she was gone more than she was home.

T. S. Kincaid

Every other night I'd see a different car drive up. She'd always forget to tell me good-bye 'fore she left and she and the babysitter'd always have a fight. It was never 'bout money though, she seemed to have lots of that. As a matter of fact, she all of a sudden had lots of nice things. New dresses, and hats, and lots of pretty necklaces and earbobs. She said all her new friends gave'em to her. I thought that was awful nice, though I wish they woulda got me somethin' once in a while. They never did.

Then, one time, Miss Baxter was watchin' me, and mama didn't come home for two whole days. Boy, Miss Baxter was mad as a hornet when she did get back. She told Mama, never again.

"Well, why the hell not? Was he trouble? If so, I'll bust his ass!" Mama promised.

"*He* is not the problem!" Said Miss Baxter.

"Then what's the problem?" Mama wanted to know.

"He's not my kid. He's yours. Why don't you start actin' like a mother and stay home for once?"

"How dare you tell me what to do! You get out of here and don't ever come back."

"Oh, don't worry, honey, I won't!" Miss Baxter slammed the door.

I'M TIMMY

The next day at school I heard Miss Baxter talkin' to one of the teachers, "She ain't gonna be able to find nobody to keep him. Everybody's 'fraid she's gonna run off sometime and never come back."

I wasn't for sure she was talkin' 'bout mama, cause she got all quiet when she saw me standin' there.

Lots of nights, I begged Mama not to go, but she would just say, "Oh, leave me alone. I have a right to go out and have a little fun. I ain't an old maid, you know."

"Oh no! Mama," I'd tell her, 'You're the prettiest girl in the world."

Don't tell nobody, but a time or two I heard mama sneak out of the house after I'd gone to bed. She didn't have no babysitter at all. I was so scared. I cried a lot, and would run through the house and turn on all the lights, sos I wouldn't have to be in the dark. Mama would come home and be spittin' nails after seein' all them lights on.

She'd yell, "Timothy! What the hell? Do you think I own the power company?"

After that she'd lock my door 'fore she left. I'd still turn my light on, but on nights when I had to go to the bathroom, man it was rough.

T. S. Kincaid

Promise you won't say nothin'? More than once, I would have to pull that curtain back, and pee in the closet. I don't think mama ever knowed about that, cause if she did she never said.

I hated when mama went out. I missed her somethin' awful. I knowed there was no way I was gonna make mama see how I felt. When she got somethin' on her mind that she wanted to do, couldn't nobody stop her.

One day, when I'd just got on the bus and sat down, Eddie hollered, "Hey, Timmy! My daddy said to tell your Mama he'd be glad to pay for a piece of that."

"A piece of what?" I asked.

Eddie just laughed and said, "Just tell her he said he'd be glad to."

"Me, too," Chester mumbled, as he was drivin' away.

I had no idea what they was talkin' bout. They must all be crazy, thinkin' my Mama made cakes or somethin'. My mama don't bake. Anyways, when I went home and told mama what they said her eyes looked like fire was gonna fly out of 'em. She told me to tell that boy to go to hell.

I'M TIMMY

Then, one day, it happened. I got off the bus and saw two scuffed up suitcases sittin' on the front porch. My heart started beatin' real fast as I ran inside the trailer.

"Mama?"

I ran to every room. But no mama. I got scared and tears filled my eyes.

"Mama?" I yelled again. I couldn't find her anywhere.

Her pretty clothes and jewelry looked like some was missin'.

I sat down in the middle of the floor and screamed!

All the sudden, the back door swung open and there was mama carryin' in another suitcase.

"What the hell is wrong with you?" she yelled.

"Mama!" I was so happy I 'bout jumped out of my skin. "What're you doin?"

"Packin." She said.

My eyes grew wide. No way! Not in a million years did I ever think my mama would leave me. I stood there as the tears rolled down my cheeks.

"Oh! Mama! Please don't go,"I begged.

"I'm not leavin' you, you dumbass. We're moving."

"Movin'? Really? Where we goin'?"

T. S. Kincaid

Wait this was all happenin' so fast. I had to stop for a minute.

"We're movin' to Kentucky. Now hurry up and get your things packed. We gotta bus to catch."

"To Kentucky? To live with Mawmaw Pike again? Yippee!" I hollered so loud, I know all the neighbors could hear.

"Now, we are just gonna stay there for a little while, 'till I can find a place. You hear?"

I heard, but I didn't care. I didn't care if it was for one night or a thousand years. We were movin'. And I was gonna get to see my mawmaw again and that made me happy inside.

I jumped so high I fell over on my back.

"Get up, you idiot! Don't break your leg before we leave." Mama growled.

I ran to my room and packed as fast as I could. It didn't take long 'cause I don't have much. Just a few shirts and some britches and underwear. Mama gave me the smallest suitcase. She stuffed most of her things in the other one she carried in from the shed, plus the two on the porch. She said she was only takin' her best things' and someone else could have the rest.

Pretty soon, Uncle Bob drove up to take us to the Greyhound Bus Station.

I'M TIMMY

It was a quiet ride, cept for Uncle Bob askin,' "You sure you wanna do this?"

"Ain't got much choice," Said Mama. "Sides. I'm getting' tired and want to settle down and get a place of my own."

"You mean for you and Timmy, right?"

"Yeah, yeah, whatever." Mama said.

When we heard them say our bus was ready to go, Uncle Bob looked at me and told me to be good. I said I would. Things just wasn't the same between me and him since that day Daddy died and he hit me. He told Mama bye and gave her a kiss an' a hug. I seen him slip somethin' into her hand, but I don't know what it was. She stuffed it in her pocket.

The bus rolled out of the station just as the sun was settin'. It was the prettiest sunset I ever seen. This was the best day of my life. The houses and streetlights flashed by like a dream, taking me and mama further and further away from Eddie and Beau, my school, and the little town of Raymond.

I scooched in real close to Mama who pushed me away and turned me towards the winda. I stayed in that spot all night long. Watchin' all those lights 'til I finally fell asleep. Dreamin' that now all my troubles was over, and we was gonna be so happy in our new home.

Chapter 7

I FORGOT TO tell you one more thing about movin' back to Kentucky and livin' with Mawmaw Pike. And this was the best part. when we got there, it was almost time for school to be out, and mama told me I didn't have to go to my new school 'til next year.

I loved livin' with my mawmaw. Her house's so nice and cozy. She kept teachin' me about the birds, and I'm real good at namin' most of 'em now. My favorite is the mockin' bird. You're not gonna believe this, but I swear it's true. One time me and mawmaw was sittin' out on her back porch and we heared a police car siren. Mawmaw said the police must be lookin' for somebody. That siren sounded like it was all over the place and mawmaw and me kept lookin' up and down the road.

Finally, Mawmaw said, "well, Timmy, would you look at that? That little booger's been sittin' here this whole time 'tendin' like he was a siren."

I looked up and seen a mockin' bird sittin' on a branch as pretty as you please.

Me and Mawmaw laughed and laughed 'bout that.

Thing's is good here.

I'm happy.

Mawmaw's even been lettin' me help in her garden. I get to pick all the vegetables when they're ready. We got corn, cucumbers, lettuce, carrots, green beans, and my favorite, tomatoes. Have you ever had a real garden tomatoe? Not them store bought kind, but a real ripe juicy mater? Boy, they's the best. I could sit and eat a whole mess of em' in one sittin'. Mawmaw says I can even help her can 'em if I slow down and they's any left.

T. S. Kincaid

Me and mama and mawmaw would all go out on the porch in the afternoons. Mawmaw would let me sit with her in the swing while I snapped beans and she peeled apples or potatoes. Mama would sit over in the rockin' chair.

"I'm so bored." Mama said as she let out a big breath.

"Well, Lord knows why Lou Ann, 'cause they's all kinds of things to do round here." Said Mawmaw.

"Like what?" Mama asked.

"Why they's tons of laundry to warsh and dustin' to do, and them dishes need to be put away, 'fore I fix supper and there's…"

"Oh! Momma! I ain't talkin' bout that!"

"Well, I am! It's 'bout time you started helpin' out a little bit around here." Mawmaw started breathin' heavy.

Mama rolled her eyes and looked down the road. She got real excited and jumped up and run towards the fence. She was a wavin' and jumpin' up and down, when this big ole green car without a top on it rolled up. Some man was sittin' in it.

He looked at mama and asked her if she'd like to go for a ride.

"You bet I would!" she said.

'Fore we knowed it, mama was in that car.

"What about supper?" Mawmaw asked.

"I'll get it later. Don't wait up!" And off she went.

Mama went out a lot after that. I could hear her and mawmaw fussin' late at night when she'd get home.

"You're gonna have to start helpin' me, Lou Ann. I can't keep up with all this extra work. You're gonna have to find a job or somethin'. Timmy's eatin' me out of house and home. Lord knows where he puts it all."

"Well, stop feedin' him so much!" Mama said.

"Oh, Lou Ann, be serious. He's a growin' boy. Alls I'm sayin' is it would be nice if you stayed home once in a while, or we had a little extra income comin' in. Thing's is tight."

"Well, I told you," Mama said, "That insurance money should be comin' in any time now."

"In the meantime,what're we supposed to do?"Mawmaw'd ask.

Mama'd just go in the bathroom and slam the door.

T. S. Kincaid

On night's when mama did come home, she'd be real quiet and slip into bed. We shared a bed now that we was livin' at mawmaw's. That was just fine by me. I liked layin' there listenin' to mama sleep. I'd scootch up next to her and I could smell her pretty perfume. She always smelled so good, even when she smelled like cigarettes and beer. There was just somethin' about the way she smelled all together that I loved.

I 'member the first night we was here. I was so excited. I jumped up in the bed, and got all snuggly under the covers.

Mama came and laid down. She rolled over, and I thought she was gonna hug me, but instead, she grabbed my face and said, "Listen here, you little shit. The first time you piss on me, you're ass is gonna be in that floor so fast you won't know what hit you! You understand me?"

"Yes ma'am," I said . I knowed she meant it.

So far, I ain't had to get in the floor.

There's somethin' else I forgot to tell ya. This here's the excitin' part. There's a little river that runs right side mawmaw's house. It's more like a creek really, but when it rains real heavy, I think it's more like a river.

I'M TIMMY

Anyways, we sure have been gettin' lots of rain. I mean tons. Mawmaw says it's good for the garden if'n it don't warsh away all the soil.

I love to play in the creek, sides collectin' the chicken eggs, it's one of my favorite things to do.

You won't believe all of the critters I find. Once, I found a great big snappin' turtle. It was a hissin' and sittin' right on the edge of the water.

I went to pick it up, and mawmaw came runnin' outside sayin' "Timmy! Don't touch that! That'll bite your fingers off!"

"Bout that time, that turtle turned 'round and hissed at me again. Mawmaw came runnin' over and picked up a big ole stick. You're not gonna believe this, but that there turtle snapped that big stick like it was breakin' a toothpick. I kid you not. Woowee! If that'd been me, I probally wouldn't have no arm right now.

I find all kinds of things here in the creek. Today it's runnin' real fast and high. The fastest I ever seen.

"Timmy! Get away from that creek. That water is too high and swift today." Mawmaw yelled from the kitchen winda.

"Yes ma'am," I said.

I was gettin' ready to go back to the house when I thought I seen somethin' come rushing down with the water. It looked like some kind of poke. It got stuck on a branch just a little ways out from that rock. Was it movin'? No. That was just the water movin' it. No wait! It did move! Oh my gosh! I have to get that sack.

First, I thought 'bout gettin' mawmaw, but that might take too long, and what if

the water rushed by and warshed it away?

Then I thought about Sheba, and how I wished time and time again that I had saved her. But this wasn't Sheba. Maybe there weren't nothin' at all in that sack. Maybe it was just my 'magination. But, what if it weren't my 'magination? What if there was somethin' in there? Then I heard somethin'! Honest. I know you're probally thinkin' how, cause the water was so loud, but I'm sure of it.

If I could just get over to that rock, then I was sure I could reach out and grab it. The rock was soakin' wet and it sure was slippery. I had to be extra careful. Maybe, just maybe, if I stretched real far, I could grab onto that branch. Whoops, I slipped again. I looked around an found a long stick, but when I reached the sack, it was real heavy and my stick broke. Darn!

Now, I had to think real fast. What if I walked around the rock and tried to reach it from there? I took my time but went as fast as I could. I felt my boot sink down into the mud, but that's okay, I weren't goin' nowhere. Then, I stretched and pulled that tree branch, just as hard as I could. I was really thinkin' hard and tryin' my best 'cause I was stickin' my tongue out. You probally would'a laughed if you could'a seen me.

I got it!! I got it!

Whoa! I grabbed that sack and held on tight. 'Bout that time that water rushed by me so fast. I thought for sure it was gonna come over my head and take me down the stream with it.

I tried to pull my leg out, but my boot was still stuck in the mud. I tried pullin' real hard again, but it was like it was suckin' on my foot.

"Mawmaw!" I screamed! "Mawmaw, help me!"

I screamed it over and over.

Finally, I looked up and saw mawmaw come runnin' with a broom.

This ain't no time for sweepin' I thought.

But mawmaw knowd what she was doing 'cause she stuck it over to me and said,

"Here, Timmy, grab on!"

"Take this here sack first!" I yelled.

"There's no time to argue, now grab on!" Mawmaw hollered.

But there was no way I was gonna have to live with another thing like what happened to Sheba. Finally, she grabbed the sack and tossed it in the yard behind her. I grabbed hold of that broom and held on for dear life.

She pulled and tugged and I pulled and tugged until finally that suction broke loose and I fell on top of Mawmaw as she fell back on the bank. We was both out of breath.

I hurried and crawled to the sack as fast as I could. Mawmaw was still layin' there.

"Oh, Timmy! You nearly scared the life outta me."

I ran back over to her and said, "Look Mawmaw, there is somethin' in this sack'."

Mawmaw tried to untie the knot, but said, "Here you do it, my hands are too sore."

I pulled and tugged as best I could, 'til I finally got it open. I told mawmaw I couldn't look and to look for me.

She pulled the edges apart and peeked inside. I knew from her eyes before she said anythin'.

"Oh! The poor little things."

"What is it Mawmaw?" I asked. I finally looked and sucked in my breath.

"Who would do such a thing?" I said as the tears welled up in my eyes.

"Someone who is completely heartless, honey." Mawmaw answered.

Someone like Eddie and Beau, I thought. But they was hundred's of miles away. I learned that day that there was meanness everywhere.

"Come on, let's see if we can't find an old bin to bury these little ones in."

I put my arms around that sack, and toted it back up to the house. I asked mawmaw if I could lay it on the kitchen counter,but she said to just put it on the table. It was dirty and muddy, but she didn't care.

My heart was broken.

Then, I swear, I heard the tiniest little meow.

"Mawmaw! I think one of 'ems still alive."

"Hurry, child bring it to me." She ordered.

We laid that sack down on the floor and picked out all five kittens. Mawmaw carefully checked every one of 'em.

"No child! I'm sorry."

"I know I heard it. It weren't my 'magination. Check again." My eyes begged.

I picked up two at a time, and all of the sudden the one layin'on the floor, I seen it! I seen it's tiny head move.

I put the other ones down and grabbed it up. " See?"

Mawmaw grabbed a clean dish towel from the drawer and wrapped it up nice and warm.

"Here, Timmy, take her while I warm up some milk. Easy, not too tight now, put her up 'round your neck."

I held her close. She let out a quiet little cry.

"Oh, you poor little dumplin', " said Mawmaw as she dipped a washcloth into the warm milk. "Here, Timmy, put a little bit on her lips."

"Mawmaw! That's the perfect name. Since we found her dumped in the creek, we'll call her Dumplin. Can I keep her?"

"That's up to your mama, honey. After all, she's the one gonna have to feed it and make sure it stays healthy. Chances are she'll say, 'no.' People are funny 'bout cats. Cats are like children, adorable when they're little, but can be a real pain in the ass when they grow up. It takes a special person to love a cat."

Then I thought I must be the most special person in the world, cause I was for sure in love with Dumplin'.

I'm Timmy

I was in the bedroom with Dumplin' when Mama came in.

"What the hell is that?" She looked disgusted.

I held up the box, "It's a kitten, Mama. Ain't she the cutest thing you ever seen? Please, Mama, can I keep her?"

"Not just no! but hell no!" Mama said."You're not keepin' that flea-bitten varmit. Now take it right back where you got it from."

"I can't, Mama; she was in the creek; someone dumped her there. Please, Mama, please can't I keep her?"

"You heard what I said, Timothy."

I dropped my shoulders and lowered my head.

"Now wait a minute, Lou Ann, this here's *my* house and I say the kitten can stay. Why do you always have to be so mean to the boy?"

Mama looked over at me, then back to mawmaw.

"This may be *your* house Momma, but *I'm* the boss of Timothy. Now get that damn kitten out of my sight and I never wanna see it again."

The tears in my eyes was makin' 'em all blury as I carried the box to the kitchen. Mawmaw Pike followed me.

"I just can't get rid of her, Mawmaw," I whispered, " I just can't"

"Give me the box, Timmy, I'll take care of this."

I put the box down on the table and ran to my room. I threw myself on the bed and cried like you wouldn't believe.

Mama came in from the bathroom. She walked over to her make-up table and started combin' her hair.

"Stop that cryin,' or I'll give you somethin' to cry about! It's just a stupid cat."

"She's more than that," I sniffed. "She was my friend."

"Oh, please. Leave it to you, you weirdo; the only friend you got is a cat."

That made me cry even worse. I wanted Dumplin' so bad. Didn't mama care how sad I was? I was so lonely and when we found Dumplin' and she was safe, I thought she could be my special friend.

Mama put on her sweater and walked out the door.

"Timmy, Timmy, wake up, honey."

I rolled over and opened my eyes. Mawmaw reached over and turned on the light.

"Come with me, I have somethin' to show ya."

I squinted my eyes. They had to get used to the light. "What is it?"

I followed mawmaw to her room. I looked around but, didn't see nothin' different.

I rubbed my eyes.

"Look under the bed." She told me.

"Why? Are you hidin' somethin'?" Then I thought she must be wantin' me to get her her shoes or somethin'.

I looked and sure enough there was a shoebox. I slid it out from under the bed, but then I seen there was a blanket in the place of shoes. I lifted up the blanket and there was Dumplin'.

"Oh! Mawmaw, you saved her! Thank you so much." I hugged my mawmaw and smiled from ear to ear. Then I started bitin' my nails.

"What are we gonna tell mama?"

"Well," said Mawmaw. "I got it all figured out. You'll stay in my room from now on. That way you can take care of the cat 'til she is old enough to go outside. This'll be our little secret. "

But won't mama wonder why all the sudden I wanna stay in here with you?"

"We'll just tell her that you stay in here most of the time anyways, 'specially since she's mostly gone and

you don't like sleepin' by yourself. That way, you can
stay in here and she can have the bed all to herself on
the nights she does come home."

It sounded like a swell plan to me.

That summer was the best summer of my life.

Dumplin' grew fast and was so smart. She acted
like a baby ducklin' followin' it's mama around, ceptin'
she was a kitty, and I'm a boy.

She'd go with me to get the vegetables from the
garden and collect the eggs. She'd chase after the
chickens but never catch 'em. I'll tell you one thing she
was good at catchin' was mice. I'd wake up some
mornings, and there'd be a mouse layin' right side my
head on my pillow. Mawmaw said as much as she hated
that she couldn't get mad at her 'cause that was
Dumplin's way of sayin' she loved me. It felt so good
to be loved.

One thing mawmaw didn't like was Dumplin'
killin' the birds.

" I ain't gonna stand for that, Timmy."

"I ain't gonna have to get rid of her am I?" I was so
scared.

I'm Timmy

"No, we ain't gonna get rid of her, but you will have to make her wear this."

She took a collar with a little bell out of her apron pocket and put it around Dumplin's neck. My Mawmaw thinks of everything.

Mama was gone more and more that summer. When she did come round I would take Dumplin' and hide. She didn't even seem to notice I was gone. If she did, she never said nothin'. She'd just run in, take a quick shower, change her clothes, and be gone again.

When it came time for Dumplin' to move outside for good, Mawmaw helped me make her a nice bed to sleep in under the porch.

On cool summer nights, she'd fix a pallet for me on the porch and let me and Dumplin' sleep together. She'd sit out in her rocker with us and tell stories of what it was like when she was a little girl.

"You know, Timmy, I had a little kitten once. Ceptin' she was gray, not a tabby like Dumplin'. I called her Cinders. Oh, my, she was the silliest cat you ever seen. She'd run 'round in circles chasin' her tail. Then when she'd catch it, she'd take a big bite, and turn 'round and do it all over again. I'm tellin' you, that was one crazy cat."

Mawmaw got real quiet and grabbed her stomach.

"Mawmaw, you alright?'

"Yes, honey. I just got a little pain is all. Well, I reckon' it's time for bed."

"But, it's still light out. We goin' to bed this early?" I asked.

"I'm awful tired, honey, I don't know what's wrong, but I'm just plum tuckered out here lately."

I didn't want to say nothin,' but I seen that Mawmaw was gettin' tired a lot here lately too. Lots of mornin's I was up 'fore she was. And 'stead of fixin' her wonderful pancakes, she started makin' me cereal. She also started takin' naps right in the middle of the day. I knowed she was hurtin' too, 'cause I seen her take the apirin out of that little tin she kept in her apron pocket.

"You think Mama'll be home tonight?" I asked.

"I don't look for her to be. Feels like rain though, so you'ins better sleep inside tonight."

Funny how I could always smell the rain, but mawmaw said she could feel it in her bones.

Once we got settled and Dumplin' was in her bed at the foot of ours, I turned to mawmaw and said, "I love you."

"I love you too, child."

I'M TIMMY

Mornin's was for the sound of the chirpin' birds, but nights was for the sound of crickets and the croakin' frogs beside the tricklin' creek. Between them sounds and the sounds of mawmaw snorin', I knowed all was right, as I fell asleep.

Chapter 8

"COME ON TIMMY, or we'll be late."

Mawmaw was already dressed and had her hat on.

"Where we goin'?" I asked.

"We just have to go uptown for a spell" Mawmaw said.

I hurried and got dressed and after I brushed my teeth I said, "Are we takin' the bus?"

"No, it's such a nice day, I thought we'd walk."

I'm Timmy

I liked walkin' with mawmaw. She always showed me things I'd never notice if I was lookin' on my own. Like the kinds of flowers growin' in the yards we passed by. Or the types of clouds in the sky. She knowed so much 'bout everythin'.

"Mawmaw, how'd you get so smart? I bet you went to school for a long time, huh?"

"Me? Oh no, child. I only went to third grade."

"'Hey, that's the grade I'm gonna be in." I said.

"Yes," Said Mawmaw, "in less than two weeks."

I was excited and dreadin' it all at the same time. I wanted to go to school, 'cause I liked learnin', but on the other hand, I didn't want to leave Dumplin' and mawmaw.

"But to answer your question, Timmy. I got as smart as I am by readin'."

"Readin' makes you smart?" I couldn't believe it.

"Why, yes, honey. If you can read, you can learn all kinds of things. Readin' and noticin' what's goin' on 'round you. You got to use all of your senses. It's a great big world out there. And if you can read, you can learn 'bout all kinds of things you'd never know 'bout otherwise. Yessir, learnin' to read and to keep readin' is the most important thing in life."

T. S. Kincaid

"I thought love was the most important thing, Mawmaw."

She looked at me real strange like. Finally she said, "I guess you're right, honey. Love, then readin'.''

We walked and talked on down that street, til we come to a big buildin'.

"This here's a doctor's office," I said. "What are we doin' here? Somebody sick?"

"Well, I been feelin' kinda poorly, so I thought I'd come see him. Now I want you on your best behavior, ya hear?"

"Yes'ma'am," I said.

The doctor's office was nice, It had lots of wooden chairs to sit in and it smelled clean. Not like the smell of soap I used to warsh with, but like rubbin' alcohol that mawmaw used to clean my skinned knees with. I knowd my knees sure did burn when she poured that stuff on me, and this here office kinda burned my nose.

Me and mawmaw sat down next to each other. They was some other people in there too. They all looked like mawmaw, old. We waited for a long time.

Then they called mawmaw's name. I stood up to go in with her, but she put her hand up and said, "Timmy, stay here. Now 'member what I said."

I sat back down and scootched back in my chair.

I'M TIMMY

Mawmaw said, "Oh, I almost forgot. Here."

She reached into her pocketbook and pulled out a brand new *Superman* Comic book. My face lit up like it was Christmas.

"Thanks, Mawmaw." I smiled.

I sat back down and looked at every picture on every page. I tried to read it, but for some reason, it seems like I get my letters all mixed up and can't make a lotta sense out of 'em. Mawmaw said she seen that too, and that was somethin' the teacher in my new school was gonna be able to help me with.

When mawmaw came back out of the office, her face had changed. She looked real worried and I kept askin' her what was wrong, but she wouldn't give me no answer. Then I tried to talk to her about the new comic she got me and I thanked her again for it. But she was still quiet. Like she was thinkin' real hard 'bout somethin'.

By the time we got home, Mawmaw went straight to bed. I guess she was all tuckered out from all that walkin'. That's the first time I can 'member she didn't fix no supper. That was all right though, 'cause I made peanut butter and jelly sandwiches for us instead.

T. S. Kincaid

Hard to believe these past two weeks just flew by. Tomorrow I start my new school. Mawmaw sat me down in the kitchen and gave me a haircut just like Daddy used to wear.

"My, my, I never noticed how much you look like your daddy, 'til now." Mawmaw said.

I began to cry.

 I missed Daddy.

Sometimes when I'd be sittin' out near the creek with Dumplin' I'd think of him. Mawmaw said when a person who's passed just pops in your head, that means their thinkin' of you too, and if we never forget 'em, that's like keepin' 'em alive and with us all the time.

We had a big cookout that weekend before school started. It was some kinda holiday, or somethin'. Mama came by for a little while and ate. She kept talkin' 'bout her friend, George. She said she was gonna bring him round someday and let us all meet him.

 "Don't bring him here," Mawmaw said. ""I heard he's married."

"They're separated, Momma." Mama snapped.

"Married is married." Mawmaw said.

Mama didn't seem to like that 'cause next thing I knowed she was up and leavin'. She was driving a real nice car.

I'M TIMMY

"Did you finally get your license, Mama?" I asked.

"You just mind your own business!" Mama snapped.

"Will you take me for a ride in it?" I asked again.

She said I'd get the seats dirty if I sat in 'em. Mawmaw breathed real heavy. Mama looked at her, then looked back at me and said maybe she'd take me some other time.

I sat straight up in bed. My heart was thumpin' so loud I could hear it in my ears. Mama's shadow was on the bedroom wall. It looked real big. There was another shadow of a chair, but I could'nt see who was sittin' in it.

"Keep your voice down, I said." It was mawmaw's voice who said that. She musta been the one sittin' in the chair.

But mama didn't listen.

"What the hell are you sayin' Momma?" Mama yelled.

"I already told you." Mawmaw said real quiet like.

"Well, I ain't gonna let you do it." Mama was still loud.

"You ain't got no choice, it's already been done."

I checked to make sure Dumplin' wasn't around and I sneaked up real close to the bedroom door. I didn't have no trouble hearin' mama. It was mawmaw I was havin' a hard time hearin',

"You're the biggest liar who ever lived." Mama screamed.

Had she found out about Dumplin'? I looked around in the darkness, but I couldn't find her. I sneaked over to the winda, and pulled the curtain back, but the winda was shut and locked. I tried to see out, but it was real dark, not a star in the sky. She must be out there. Maybe she was up under the porch. I crawled back over to the bedroom door and kept listen'.

Mama was sayin' all kinds of mean things to Mawmaw. It made me feel sick inside.

"Look Lou Ann, I know what I told you, but I ain't got no choice. I need this operation. And the only way to pay for it is to sell the house. Don't you understand?"

My mouth dropped. I couldn't believe it!

"Well, what am I supposed to do? You promised me I could have this house and now you done sold it out from under me."

Mawmaw said somethin' I couldn't hear.

"Well, you're gonna die anyways. So what good did it do to sell this house? You'll be dead and I'll still have nothin'. Thanks a lot, Momma!"

I'M TIMMY

I couldn't bear to hear no more. I crawled back into bed and pulled the covers up real close. I jumped when the door slammed and I heard the car screech away. I climbed out of bed and ran to Mawmaw. We both hugged each other and cried.

Mawmaw wiped my eyes. "Listen, Timmy, I have somethin' important to talk to you about. I havn't been feelin' very well, and the doctor said I need an operation."

"But, you're gonna be okay, right?"

"Well, of course, honey. But the point I am tryin' to make is that operations are very expensive. The only way I could pay for it was to put this house up for sale."

"But, if you're gonna be okay, where are you gonna live if you ain't got no house no more?" I asked.

"Well, that's just it. See, after my operation, I'm gonna live in a place where other folks like me…"

"You mean older?"

"Um, well, yes. But anyway, that's where I will live from now on."

"Oh," I said. "I see. Mawmaw, if I had the money I'd give it to ya."

"Oh, I know you would, honey. I just wanted to explain things to you sos you'd understand."

"I understand." I lied. " But Mawmaw, if you sell this house and go to live somewheres else, where will I live?"

"With your Mama, of course."

I have to be honest, I liked that idea. I missed my mama. It would be nice to spend more time with her.

Mawmaw told me to try and get some rest, cause I had a big day tomorrow. That's right, tomorrow I'd be starting school.

The next mornin' I got up early to go lookin' for Dumplin.'"Here, Kitty. Kitty," I hollered.

I looked everywhere, even down by the creek, but I couldn't find her. I was worried to death. Mawmaw finally came out and got me and said, "Timmy, honey, you're gonna be late for school."

"But Mawmaw, I can't find Dumplin.'"

"Oh, I'm sure she's fine. You go on to school and I'll look for her. I bet she'll be here by the time you get home."

I hoped so. I got on that bus and sat at the first winda I came to sos I could look out and see if I spotted her. As worried as I was, I got to admit that this bus ride was a lot better than the other bus rides I used to have. Do you know why? Yep, you guessed it, no Eddie or Beau. Kids on this bus seemed all right. I could tell they knowed I was new, 'cause they all seemed to know each other. But that was okay. As long as they left me alone, I was just fine.

My teacher's name was Mrs. Calhoun. She looked nice. Her hair was the color of mine, and she wore it down with a ribbon around it and flipped up on the ends When it came time for me to stand up and say my name and somethin' about myself, the only thing I could think to say was:

"My name is Timmy Thomson. My daddy's dead and me and my mama just moved here from Raymond, Mississippi. I got a cat named Dumplin' who is my best friend."

All the kids laughed at that.

Mrs. Calhoun said, "Oh, so you're from Mississippi? I don't believe their schools are as good as ours so I'm sure you are gonna have a lot of catchin' up to do."

I figured one school was just as good as the other, but I didn't say nothin'.

Then she asked me what my mother's maiden name was.

I told her, "I don't know what you mean."

She said, "Of course you don't. What I mean is, what was your Mama's last name before she married your Daddy?"

I said, "Alls I know is my mama's name is Lou Ann, but my Mawmaw Pike is her mama."

"Ah," Mrs. Calhoun said, 'I thought I saw a resemblance. I went to school with your mama; she had quite a reputation, as I recall.'

"Yes, Ma'am," I said cause I didn't know what a reputation was. I sort of got the feelin' Mrs. Calhoun didn't like me too much, but maybe that was just my 'magination.

First thing I done when I got off the bus that day was run to the house to see if Dumplin' was there. She wasn't.

Mawmaw said she looked for her, but hadn't seen her. She told me to try not to worry, that cats do that sometimes. She said, "Just be patient, she'll be back."

I waited and worried those next few weeks while Mawmaw got the house ready to turn over to the new owners.

Each day I came home there was less and less stuff in the house. I asked mawmaw where all of it'd gone.

I'M TIMMY

"Well, Timmy, I gave a lot of it to my neighbors and friends. But this weekend I'm goin' to see if I can sell the rest in a yard sale."

I'd never had no yard sale before. Mawmaw let me help color the signs and go 'round with a neighbor to put 'em up. That gave me the chance to look for Dumplin' but I never did see her.

I thought a lot about Dumplin' and where she might be. I thought a lot about Sheba too, and wondered if the same thing had happened to Dumplin'. Then I wondered if me and daddy made the right choice 'bout not tellin' that lady 'bout Sheba. Least she woulda knowed what happened even if it was so awful. I think I'd like to know. It's the not knowin', the always lookin', the always wonderin', that's awful.

The yard sale was excitin' to watch. All kinds of people came round, lookin' at mawmaw's stuff and makin' deals with her. Mawmaw called it hagglin'. In the end she made pert near eighty dollars. She said she was happy with that.

The worst day of my life came the next day. Mawmaw Pike had her suitcases all packed. She and me sat on the front porch swing.

"Mawmaw, do you have to go?"

"Yes, honey, I do." She answered.

"Can't you take me with you?" I begged.

"Oh, no child. That's no place for children."

"Can I come and visit you?" I finally asked.

"Sure you can, any time you like."

"Promise?" I looked her dead in the eye.

"Cross my heart." She promised.

I looked up into her sad eyes and asked what was I gonna do about Dumplin' now that I was gonna be movin' too.

" She won't know where to find me." I cried.

"Timmy," Mawmaw said, "Look at me. Love will always find a way. Some day you will see her again. I just know it. Now you listen to me. You be a good boy. Listen to and try to take care of your mama. She needs you." Her eyes filled with tears.

"I love you, Timothy, more than you will ever know. And I would never leave you if I didn't have to. You remember that, okay?"

I shook my head yes 'cause my throat felt all funny and I didn't think any words would come out.

I looked up and seen a car drivin' by real slow. It was the same car that mama was drivin' that day of the cook-out. I waved but she just sped off.

"Wasn't that Mama?" I asked.

I'M TIMMY

"I believe it was, Timmy. I reckon she's still mad and doesn't want to tell me bye.

She'll probally circle the block till my ride comes."

That's 'xactly what she done too, 'cause I seen her drive by a few more times.

When Mawmaw Pike got on that white bus and it started to drive away, I couldn't help but cry.

She was cryin' too. "Now, you 'member what I said. Your mama will be here to pick you up soon as I'm gone. You just wait there on the porch."

I don't know what happened to me as that bus drove away, but I started runnin' after it. I ran so hard and so fast that my legs gave out. I sat there in the middle of that street screamin' and beggin' for that bus to bring her back. But it just drove away. Takin' Mawmaw Pike and my heart with it.

Chapter 9

I FINALLY GOT up out of the street and walked back
to the porch. I sat down on the swing where I waited for
mama. I sat there for a long time. It got later and later.
I started to wonder what would happen if she never
came for me. What would I do? I couldn't go back in
the house 'cause mawmaw had locked the door when
she left. It started to get dark. I reckon I fell asleep

sittin' there waitin' cause I opened my eyes when I heard a car comin' up the drive. The headlights was bright and I couldn't see who it was.

It was mama.

I didn't know it was her at first, cause she was ridin' in a different car.

"Where you been, Mama?" I asked.

"Me and Buddy here just went and grabbed a bite to eat. You got all your stuff?"

"Yes, Ma'am. It's here on the porch," I said as I grabbed my suitcase. "Did you get me anythin'? I'm 'bout starved."

"Well, no," said Mama. "I didn't even think about it. I thought for sure you'd eat with your mawmaw 'fore she left."

"Mama, mawmaw left a long time ago. She said you'd get me somethin' to eat." I whined.

"Well, she was wrong. Now stop that whinin'! It ain't gonna kill ya to miss a meal or two."

Tears filled my eyes. I was so hungry and wore out. Her friend, Buddy, said he'd go and get me somethin' but mama told him it was okay. He'd already spent enough on us that day. I don't know why she said us, 'cause I never got nothin'.

T. S. Kincaid

Buddy took us uptown a little ways from where mawmaw had went to the doctor. He dropped us off at a set of steps that led into a buildin'. When we opened the door it led to another set of steps that went up and 'round, then up again. I had to tote that suitcase of mine all the way up them steps. I don't mind tellin' ya it was mighty heavy. I had to stop and rest a time or two. I was breathin' real hard when I made it to the top and was sure glad we didn't have no more steps to climb.

Mama opened the door at the end of the hall. She went first and flipped on the light. It was a small space with big windas. The kitchen and livin'room was all in one room and there was a little bathroom with just a sink, toilet and shower. There weren't no bathtub, and I asked mama how I was 'sposed to take a bath.

"You see that there metal tub hangin' on the wall?" She said.

I nodded.

"Well, when ya wanna take a bath, you fill that with water and take one."

It looked awful small, not nothin' like the big white bathtub with the claw feet at mawmaws.

I'M TIMMY

Man, I sure did have fun slidin'down the back of that tub into the water.It made big waves and I'd slide over and over 'til the water was almost gone. Mawmaw came in one time after I was done and told me to clean all that water up off the floor. Boy, she sure was mad. But not too mad, 'cause she told me next time don't fill it so full. Then she gave me a wink.

I won't be able to slide in this new tub.

Then mama showed me the bedroom. It was real small, just big enough for the bed. And one little closet that was way over in the corner you had to climb over the bed to get to.

I looked in the icebox for somethin' to eat, but alls that was in there was a bottle of wine and a couple of beers. I guess mama forgot to go to the grocery store.

Soon as I was settled in, mama started getting' dressed.

I asked her where she was goin' and she said, "Out."

I thought to myself, 'Oh Mama, why can't you stay home with me just once?' But I didn't dare say nothin' out loud.

She was still just as pretty as ever. I missed watchin' her get dressed and twirl around the room. She seemed to be so happy when she went out and I told myself if that was what made her happy, then it was alright by me.

As mama was leavin' I heard one of the neighbors ask her didn't she have a little boy? Mama told a big fib, and said I was stayin' with my mawmaw for a while. Maybe that was why she told me I should be quiet as a mouse and don't open the door for nobody, if'n I knowed what was good for me.

That first night was mighty scary bein' there all by myself. The sounds of the cars blowin' in the streets and sirens goin' by at all hours kept me awake. I could hear the people in the next apartment over talkin' and I could smell the food they'd cooked. The smell stayed 'round long after the food was gone. I wished I had me some.

By the end of the week, I was used to the place. I even knowed one of the kids from my school who lived in another apartment. We'd walk to the bus stop together.

Then one night I heared mama and some man comin' up the stairs. He was singin' real loud. Mama was laughin' and singin' right along with him. When they got to the door, I could hear the keys ginglin'. It took a while for her to open it. Finally, they burst in and

I'm Timmy

I heard mama tell the man shush, 'cause I was in the bedroom sleepin.'

"Well, what the hell's he doin' in there? I wanna go in there." The man said.

"We can't right now. Maybe you'd better go home." Mama told him.

"Oh, no you don't. I didn't take you out to wine and dine for nothin'. You owe me little lady, and you are gonna pay."

Mama came in and got me up and told me to get in the closet.

I didn't want to, but mama promised to whip me good if I didn't.

I got in, but left the door cracked sos I could see what was goin' on.

The man pushed mama down on the bed and started pullin' on her clothes.

"Hold on a minute, you're gonna rip it." I heard mama say.

The man started kissin' mama on the neck, tellin' her to hurry up.

"Good things comes to them that waits," Mama said.

"Oh, that's horse shit!" the man said as he grabbed at her again.

T. S. Kincaid

He tore her pretty dress. She smacked him. And he really walloped her good. I was so mad, I opened the door and jumped on his back. He grabbed me by the arms and I went flyin'. I ended up against the wall in the livin' room.

Mama started screamin' and clawin' at the man's face. He kept tryin' to pin her down and was smackin' her. She was fightin' and kickin' him with all her might. I tried to hit the man again, but every time he'd just throw me back off.

Soon the neighbors was bangin' on the door askin' if everythin' was all right.

Before I knowed it, there was a real loud knock, and a boomin' voice said, "Police! Open up!"

Mama ran for the door, but the man grabbed her and threw her against the icebox. She fell to the floor in pain. I ran to the door and opened it. Before I knowed it, the policemen was all over that man. They put him in handcuffs and dragged him down the stairs.

All the neighbors was lookin' in at mama who was still on the floor. Her hair was all messed up and her dress was ripped down the front. She had red hand marks on her face and her eyes looked like a big raccoon had drawed dark circles under 'em.

She stared at the neighbors and yelled, "What the hell are ya'll lookin' at?"

One man said, "Hey lady, we were just tryin' to help."

"Well, mind your own damn business!" Mama hollered as she slammed the door.

I ran over to mama and tried to help lift her off the floor. She was cryin' and told me to get her a cold wet warsh rag.

I got her nightgown out of the closet and helped her to bed. I asked her was she hurt.

"No, shit." Was all she said.

I snuggled up close as she would let me and listened to her cry herself to sleep. I laid there most of the night making sure that man didn't come back and that mama was okay. I like layin' there listenin' to her breathe in and out. Her soft breath made fallin' to sleep real easy.

The next mornin' my friend didn't knock on the door to walk me to the bus stop. When I got there, he just turned away from me and didn't want to talk to me. When I got on the bus, nobody wanted to sit with me. It was a long, lonely ride to school.

After lunch, I was goin' to the bathroom when I passed the teacher's lounge. I heared Mrs. Calhoun talkin' to another teacher.

"Well, serves her right. She wasn't nothin' but a little whore in high school. I guess she still is. She thought she was so hot, stealin' everybody's boyfriends. Boy, you wouldn't believe the stories I could tell you I heard about Lou Ann Pike. Now rumor has it she's runnin' all over town with any man she can find, married or not. I even heard tell she has the nerve to drive around in other women's husbands' cars."

Mrs. Calhoun looked up and seen me standin' there.

"Don't you have any manners, boy? It's not polite to eavesdrop." And she shut the door.

That evenin' when I got home from school there was a big red sign with the word EVICTION nailed on the door.

Mama was in there puttin' all her stuff in a suitcase. She told me to get my things and come on.

"Where we goin', Mama?"

"Anywhere but here." She said.

I'M TIMMY

Turns out we didn't go very far atall, just a few blocks. Mama saw a sign that said, For Rent and asked the cab driver to stop there.

She went and talked to a man who answered the door. I saw mama shake her head a time or two, then she reached inside her pocketbook and pulled out some cash. After that, she shook his hand and waved for me to come on. The cab driver got our suitcases from the trunk and carried them in for us. I was glad there weren't as many stairs this time. Only 'bout half as there was last.

When we reached the top of the stairs I could hear a little dog barkin'. A woman with curlers in her hair and big thick glasses cracked her door open and peeked out at us. Her little dog came runnin' out and ran right to me.

"Oh, hello," I said as I reached down to pet it.

It had a yappy little bark and nipped my hand when I stuck it out.

The woman ran out in her bathrobe and grabbed her dog, sayin' how sorry she was.

"Keep your damn dog away from my kid!" Mama snapped.

The woman's face turned red and she grabbed her dog sayin', "Come on, Samson. We know when we're not welcome."

She went back to her apartment and slammed the door.

"It's okay, Mama, it didn't hurt. See didn't even break the skin." I held up my hand, but mama just rolled her eyes and said somethin' about not gettin' any ideas about gettin' a damn dog.

This apartment was smaller than the last, if you can believe that. We didn't have a bedroom a tall, but each night mama would pull the bed down from the wall and we would sleep in it.

Night after night mama would tell me not to have no accidents in her bed. I'd stand at the toilet and try and try to go but it just wouldn't come out. I even turned the water on at the sink and let it drip thinkin' that would help. It didn't. I was so scared I was gonna pee, that each night when I got in the bed I would hold it and squeeze real tight 'til it hurt.

One night Mama grabbed my arm and said, " What're you doin'?"

"Nothin'" I said.

"Well, if I catch you playin' with that thing of yours, I'll cut it off, you hear me?"

"I wasn't pla.."

"Shut up and go to sleep!" Mama yelled.

Each day I would come home with all kinds of homework.

Mama'd say, "Good God, what does that woman do all day? If she thinks I'm gonna do her job for her she can forget it."

"She says I need extra work 'cause I ain't as smart as them other kids, so she gives me more than the others." I tried to tell mama.

"Oh, she's full of shit." Mama'd say. " She's just tryin' to make me look bad by givin' you all that work. Well, you tell her I said, you ain't doin' it."

When I told Mrs. Calhoun what mama said, she said, "Suit yourself. Timothy, go stand in the corner and stay there til I say you can sit down. Some days I would stand there all day. I didn't even get to go out for recess.

One day, Mr. Brown, the principal, walked by and saw me standin' there.

"What's goin' on here?" he asked.

Mrs. Calhoun stood from her desk and said that I was a problem child who refused to do my homework.

T. S. Kincaid

"Come with me young man," Mr. Brown said.

We walked down the hallway to his office. He had great big windas and I was lookin' out of them at the beautiful fall leaves. The mountains looked so pretty. All the sudden Mr. Brown told me to bend over.

I put my brows together and said, "Sir?"

"Bend over, I said. This is how we deal with problem children."

He took out a paddle and gave me three good whacks. Man did that hurt! I started cryin' and rubbin' my bottom.

"That will teach you not to do your work. Now get back to class and don't let me see you here again."

I slowly walked back to class. I wiped my eyes before I went through the door. Mrs. Calhoun looked up and smiled. "You'll learn your lessons one way or the other," she said.

I didn't tell Mama 'bout me getting' a paddlin'. I was fraid I'd get the same when I got home if I did.

Night after night she'd go out and not come home 'til well up into the mornin'.

One night, I heard the lady with the dog tellin' mama that she knowed what she was up to and that if she didn't stop leavin' me alone at nights she was gonna call the law. This made mama madder than I'd seen in a long time. She started hittin' and smackin' the lady on the arms and face. Tellin' her to get back in her apartment and keep her nose to herself.

Mama came in the apartment and started walkin' back and forth across the floor. She was talkin' like she was on the telephone, 'ceptin we ain't got one.

Next thing I knowed, the cops was there tellin' mama she couldn't be hittin' her neighbors. They said the lady said she wouldn't press charges on 'count of me, but to not let it happen again.

After they left, mama stayed up the rest of the night. Walkin' and talkin' to herself.

The next day when I come home there was another one of them notes that said EVICTION on the door. I didn't know what that word meant, but I knowed that every time I seen one of them signs, we moved.

T. S. Kincaid

Chapter 10

THE NEXT PLACE mama picked to live was a little ways outta town. I still had to go to the same school, though. I hated that. Mrs. Calhoun was on me every day. Seemed like I couldn't get a break. mama said she picked this trailer cause maybe the neighbors wouldn't be so nosey.

She was wrong.

I'M TIMMY

One night she come home late. I seen her zigzaggin' through the yard when she finally kicked off her shoes. She stumbled up on the porch and told her man friend to hurry up. He come zigzaggin' up after her. I hunched down by the wall near the livin' room. They was on the couch, when he musta said somethin' that made her mad. She slapped him across the face and started yellin' all kinds of bad words she'd beat me for sayin'. The man started yellin' back and wouldn't you know it? Before too long, them lights was flashin' outside.

This time the man left on his own. He called Mama a tease when he got in his car and drove off. One cop stayed behind. I seen him before. In fact, seems like every time Mama had any trouble he was there.

He and mama hung out in the kitchen for a while when I heared him say,

"Come on, Lou Ann, when are you gonna stop hangin' out with these losers and let me make an honest woman outta you?'

Mama laughed and said, "Oh, no, Frank! Ain't nobody gonna tell me what to do no more. Soon as that insurance settlement comes, me and Timothy's outta here."

"Oh, yeah?" Frank sounded surprised. "And just where do you think you're goin'?"

"Out west to California, of course."

Frank started laughin'.

Mama got real mad. "Well, I am goin' to California, and neither hell nor high water's gonna stop me!"

"Okay, Baby, simmer down. Just what do you think you're gonna do out there in California?"

"Oh, I don't know. Maybe become a famous singer or actress or somethin' like that." Mama's voice sounded far off and dreamy.

"Can you even sing?" Frank asked.

"Course I can," said Mama.

But you know what? This surprised me, cause I ain't ever heard Mama sing, 'cept for in the shower. Oh yeah, and when she'd sing along with the radio. I gotta say, Mama didn't sound like Patsy Cline or Doris Day, no matter how hard she tried. I never would tell her that 'cause she'd whip me good for sure.

"Besides," Mama went on, "I may not have to sing. Don't you think I'm pretty enough to be in a picture show?"

I'M TIMMY

"Sure, I do baby, that's why I want you to stop runnin' round with all these guys and settle down with a real man like me."

"You can't give me what I want." Said Mama

"Sure, I can, Baby, just try me."

It got real quiet and nobody was talkin'. I peeked around the corner and seen Frank press mama against the wall. He put his hand under her blouse and was kissin' her neck at the same time. Then mama took off her blouse and helped Frank take off his shirt. He undid his belt. I thought he was gonna whip mama with it, so I almost ran out there, but then I seen his pants go down to his ankles. Then he lifted mama up and pulled her skirt up around her waist. She wrapped her legs around him. He started movin' his hips back and forth. Mama was moanin' and bouncin' up and down.

She was leanin' up against the wall and her hair was getting' all messed up. She seemed to like what was happenin'. Then they started movin' faster and faster 'til I thought the whole trailer was gonna shake. I didn't like what Frank was doin' to mama and I wanted them to stop. I was so mad a noise came out of my mouth 'fore I knowed it.

Frank and mama looked over at me in shock.

T. S. Kincaid

"Oh shit!" yelled Mama, "You little asshole, get the hell outta here!"

I ran back down the hallway and jumped in the bed. I just knowed Mama was gonna beat me for what I'd seen.

I heard Franks' belt buckle rattle as he slid it back through his pants. Then he said somethin' I didn't hear and the door slammed as he got back in his car. I hid in the bed waitin' for mama to come and wallop me. I was so scared, I had the covers pulled up over my head. I waited, but mama didn't come. Finally, I rolled over and went to sleep.

I woke up with my face in the mattress. There was a heavy weight on my head, and I couldn't lift it. I tried real hard to turn my head. When I finally did I took a big gulp of air. Mama's hand was around the back of my neck and she turned my head again puttin' my face in the pee- soaked mattress. My face was wet and the pee filled up my nose and burned my eyes. Mama lifted her hand off me and grabbed her paddle. She hit me more times than I could count right on my butt. I put my hand behind me to block her hits but they just kept comin'. I cried and begged her to stop.

I'M TIMMY

She finally got off of me and grabbed me by my hair. She looked me dead in the eye and said, "I warned you, you piece of shit, not to piss in my bed."

Frank started comin' round more and more. Mama stopped goin' out all the time and found herself a job at a diner over in Lawrenceburg,. Each day when I got home from school, Frank would drive his patrol car up to our house and pick mama up to take her to work. I got to ride in the back of the patrol car. After we'd drop mama off, he'd let me sit up front with him and play the siren and turn on the lights. One time, Jimmy and Tommy, two boys from my class, seen me. The next day they had all kinds of questions for me. It made me feel real special, all the attention I was gettin'.

When I told Frank about it, he said he'd have to let me ride in the front more often. I liked Frank okay, but there was somethin' 'bout him that made me feel uneasy. Like he was sneaky or somethin'. He gave me the same feelin' I used to get when Eddie and Beau was around.

Then one day Frank showed me a side of him I'd dread for the rest of my life. We was ridin' 'round in his car when Frank seen a woman standin' on the corner. Soon as that woman seen him, her eyes got all big and she took off runnin' down a back alley. Me and Frank followed her in his car. She got to the end of the alley and had no place else to go. Her eyes had tears in 'em as Frank parked the car in front of her. He opened the door and told me to stay put.

That woman was so scared she started tryin' to jump the wall in front of her. She was hoppin' round like a trapped rabbit. Frank got closer to her and started smackin' her around. He grabbed her by her hair and pushed her down to her knees. She was cryin' and beggin' him to let her go. He held onto her hair and started undoin' his pants. I seen 'em drop to his knees. He pushed himself up against that woman's face. She struggled to get away. She crawled across the pavement, when he grabbed her from behind and lifted up her dress. She was still strugglin' to crawl away when he pushed her to the ground and climbed on top of her. I could see his bare butt movin' back and forth. He was goin' faster and faster 'til he finally let out a moan and slammed the womans face down on the hard road. She lay there crying, trying to put her dress back down. She finally scooted over and curled into a little ball beside the wall. Frank got back into the patrol car. He buttoned up his pants and sat there smilin' at that poor woman.

I couldn't believe or understand what I just seen. My brows closed in real tight and I just looked at Frank.

"Wh.." I started to say when Frank looked over at me. For a minute he acted like he forgot that I'd been sittin' there in that front seat. Then his face got a real mean look on it and he grabbed me by the back of my neck. He pulled me up close to him and before I knowed it, he had his pistol out and was pushin' it right up against the side of my head.

"Listen to me, you little bastard. One word to your mama or anyone else 'bout what you just saw, and I'll blow your little brains all over this car. You understand?"

I shook my head.

"What? I didn't hear you." Frank said.

"Yyyyes Sssir." I said.

Frank drove around a little longer. I sat there as quiet as I could be. We pulled in the parkin' lot of a little store. Frank got out and waved to the men sittin' outside on the bench. They all waved back and talked about him as he went inside.

"He's a good ole boy," they said.

"Yeah, comes from good people. I knowed him since he was knee-high to a grasshopper. He sure makes his momma proud."

I was thinkin' if they only knowed what I did.

Frank came back out of the store with a big bottle of beer and a candy bar.

He said, "Here boy, I got ya somethin'" as he threw the candy bar at me.

"Ain't ya gonna say thanks?" He asked.

I just shook my head and put on a fake smile.

By the time we got back to my house it was late. I went straight to mine and Mama's room.

Frank asked me if I wanted to stay up with him a while, but I told him I was real tired.

He said, "Okay then, suit yourself."

I laid in that bed of ours and said to myself, this was worse than I thought. Not only was Frank a lot like Eddie and Beau, he was worser. The scary part was, that he was right chere in the house, instead of just three blocks, or hundreds of miles down the road.

Chapter 11

MY EIGHTH BIRTHDAY came and went. Mama and me was talkin' one day and I said somethin' 'bout Halloween. Mama looked at the calendar and said, "Oh shit!"

"What's the matter, Mama?"

"Oh, nothin'. Your birthday was last Tuesday. I guess I forgot," Mama said.

I kinda pouted and felt like cryin'.

"Now you dry it up right now, Timothy. Just 'cause I forgot your birthday ain't no big deal. You ain't no baby no more, so don't start actin' like one. Besides, I'll make it up to you at Halloween. What kind of costume would you like and I'll see if I can get it."

"Really, Mama? You mean it?"

I was so happy. I only had to think about it for a second and knew 'xactly who I wanted to be. Can you guess? That's right, Superman.

"I said we'll see." Mama reminded me.

The day of Halloween we had a big party at school. I didn't wear my costume, 'cause mama hadn't got it yet. She said she'd try to bring it home after work. She said she was gettin' off early that day.

I got off the bus and ran as fast as I could. I opened the door and seen a package sittin' on the table, As I ripped it open, I yelled, "It's a bird, it's a plane, it's a big green dress?"

I stood there tryin' to figure out what it was when mama come from the bathroom. Her hair was all done up in curls, and she had on a skirt so big she hardly got through the door.

"Mama? What's this?"

"Why, that's my costume, silly."

I looked all around and under the table.

"Where's mine?" I asked.

"Yours? Well, fiddle dee dee, I guess I forgot." She was talkin' real funny. She walked over and put the rest of the green fringed dress on.

"You mean, you didn't get me no costume?" I started to choke up.

"Now don't you start. I had to have somethin' to wear to the party tonight, and after I found this perfect dress for me, I couldn't afford anything else."

I took a deep breath.

"That's okay," I said. "I don't mind bein' a ghost again this year."

"Oh no!" Mama said. "You ain't cuttin' up no more of my sheets."

"Well, what can I go as?" I asked.

"Nothin', "said Mama.

"Nothin'?" I asked.

"No since in worryin' bout it when you ain't goin'."

"Ain't goin'?"

"What are you a Mima bird? Why you keep repeatin' everythin' I say? I have a party to go to. Therefore, you ain't goin'."

"But you promised."

"I most certainly did not, you liar. I said, 'We'll see', And this is what we see. That you ain't goin'."

I went to my room and shut my door. I tried not to cry, but I did.

Mama told me to stay put and not go out anywhere if I knowed what was good for me.

"Don't you turn on no lights either, we don't want no ghosts or goblins comin' here."

I sat there in the dark that night. Watchin' all the other children run around in their costumes. Getting' candy, and playin' tricks. I seen some boys throw toilet paper up in a big tree.

Man they was havin' a time.

I wished I weren't so scared. I wish I was bigger and stronger and not afraid mama was gonna wallop me every time I turned around. I wish I could get mad and not be afraid to show it. I have the right to be mad, don't you think? Instead of sittin' here rockin' and bitin' my nails in the dark.

I'M TIMMY

It was getting' near Thanksgivin' and school would be on break soon. I was so glad. I needed a break. I thought 'bout Mawmaw Pike and her good cookin'. I was hopin' to see her, but mama never said nothin' 'bout it. She said I might as well forget 'bout Mawmaw Pike since she abandoned us.

I sure did miss her. I tried not to think about her, or daddy or Dumplin'. Besides Mama, they was the only things I ever loved. Not havin' 'em 'round broke my heart. Sometimes, I missed them so much that I would get sick and throw up. When that happens I just try to do like daddy said to do about Sheba, and try not to think about it. It sure is hard though.

Just before school let out on that last day before break, Mr. Brown come to the classroom. He said, "Timothy, get your things and come to my office."

My heart sank. What'd I done now?

To my surprise, there was mama. I got so scared

"What's wrong?" I asked her. I thought somethin' bad happened.

Mama just smiled real big and said, "Nothin.' I got a big surprise for you."

I was so excited I tried real hard to think what it could be.

"Are we movin' again?" I asked.

"Maybe," Mama smiled.

"Are we goin' to California? Or to see Mawmaw?"

"Just shut up and wait and see," I could tell mama was gettin' tired of my questions.

When we walked through the front door of the school building, I saw the prettiest red and white car I ever seen. Mama said it was a brand new 1955 Chevy as she ran over to it and sat on top of the hood. She looked like she was posin' for a photo.

"What do you think?" She smiled.

My eyebrows went together.

"That settlement finally came in! Woo hoo! I got me five thousand dollars."

I started jumpin' 'round yippin' and hollorin' 'til I come around to the side of the car and saw Frank getting' out of the drivers side.

"And guess what else?" Mama asked holdin' up her hand. She started wigglin' her fingers around and I could see a ring with a little shiny stone in it.

"I got me a new car and you got you a new daddy. We went down to the courthouse today and got hitched."

I'M TIMMY

My mouth dropped.

"Now you can call him, Daddy Frank, 'cause he said he ain't never gonna be your real daddy, but he won't mind you callin' him that."

My eyes filled with tears.

Mama lowered her voice and bent down to my ear and said, "Now I know he ain't like your Daddy, but Frank's been real good to us and..."

"For Crissake woman, get in the damn car. He's just a kid. You ain't gotta explain nothin' to him." Frank snapped.

Mama opened the car door and I climbed in the back seat. I scootched up toward the back of Mama and Frank's seat and put my elbows between them.

Frank pressed on the gas hard and the car sped off so fast I flew into the back seat and hit my head. Frank peered at me through his mirror and grinned.

I tried to shake off the pain and slid over to the corner between the seat and the car door. I gritted my teeth and didn't say a word. Frank pushed the gas pedal to the floor, and with each curvy turn, I was thrown around like a kid on a carnival ride.

Finally, Mama said, "Slow down! You're gonna kill somebody!"

Frank slammed on the brakes, which made the car skid sideways 'fore comin' to a stop.

"Hey!" He yelled, pinchin' mama's face so hard it made her lips squeeze into a W. "Don't you ever tell me what to do! You understand?"

Mama's eyes got real red as he jerked his hand away. She turned her head towards her side door and put her hand over her face. She didn't say nothin' after that.

That was the longest, scariest, ride of my life. Each time we turned a curve, my stomach flopped and I felt like I was gonna throw up. Boy, I knowed the beatin' I would get if I do. So I just held on for dear life and tried to take deep breaths from the open air that blastin' in my face.

I knowed now we was in trouble for sure. Now that Mama had married Frank, we would never be rid of him. Oh Daddy, if you can hear me, please help us.

Frank parked the car on the back street behind the ally. I followed Mama up the steps and onto the porch of a tan and brown house.

"I thought we was goin' home," I said.

I'M TIMMY

"We are home." Mama didn't sound too happy. "Frank's place is a little bigger than ours, so we're gonna live here from now on."

We moved so many times that I figured one place was just as good as the other. Mama opened the door, and I walked in the dark room. It smelled real musty and like old cigarettes. When my eyes finally got used to the darkness, I seen that the kitchen and livin' room was all one big space. 'Ceptin there was a counter 'fore you got to the kitchen. There was a door leadin' to what I figured was a bedroom and another side door with a small winda that looked like it went outside. I peeked through that winda and saw a small yard with a nice size oak tree.

"Wow! What a great place for a tire swing," I said.

Mama said, "We'll see."

The next thing I noticed was the Television. We ain't never had one before. I was real excited about that. Now when the boys at school talked about watchin' The Twilight Zone, I Love Lucy, and Loonie Tunes, I knowed what they was talkin' bout.

I could tell mama weren't listenin' to nothin' I said. She was still standin' at the doorway and I couldn't figure out why she wouldn't come on in. Frank came up on the porch and walked right past her.

T. S. Kincaid

Mama put her hands on her hips and said, "Hey you, aren't you forgettin' somethin'?'

Frank looked at Mama and said, "Don't tell me you expect me to carry your ass over that thre';/[
I come home one time and some woman was there. I seen her comin' out of the bedroom buttonin' up her shirt. She looked at me and smiled. Frank came out of the bedroom behind her.

The woman got her pocketbook and went to the door.

"See ya next week?" she turned and asked.

"Of course," said Frank.

After the woman walked on down the street, I asked who she was.

"None of your damn business!" Frank said. He took a drink of his beer.

"Is she a friend of Mama's?"

Frank's face got that same mean look on it again.

Next thing I knew that beer bottle come flyin' past my head. It broke all to pieces on the wall behind me.

"I thought we had an understandin'", Frank said. "Next time, that will be your head bustin' up against that wall. So, if I was you, I'd keep my damn mouth shut."

I did.

I'M TIMMY

I come home one evening and I could hear mama yellin' all the way from the bus stop. A plate flew past my arm as I opened the door.

"You still haven't answered me. How the hell could you get suspended? What did you do?"

Mama's face was red and she was breathin' real hard. I could tell they musta been fightin' for a long time.

Frank sat on the couch drinkin' his beer. He was so calm it was scary. He looked at Mama with glassy eyes and said, "I told you, that somebitch chief of mine has it in for me. I don't know why. I didn't do nothin'."

Mama squinted her eyes and I could tell she didn't believe him. For some reason, she decided to end the fight though. I was glad. I hate it when people fight.

"I guess, much as I hate to, I'll just have to pick up more shifts at the diner." Mama huffed.

I started bitin' my nails. Just the thought of spendin' more time with Frank made me nervous.

"Quit that!" Mama said as she jerked my hand out of my mouth. "You're gonna get worms."

I couldn't help it. Worms or not, bitin' my nails made me feel better.

Every day was the same. Mama was gone and Frank would want to fight.

"Come here you little pussy, put your hands up."

He cheated. He would put his palm on my head and he knowed he was too far away he'd tell me, "Swing, you little bastard, swing."

I'd swing my arms, stretchin' em as far as I could, but I never could hit him.

Then, fore I knowed it, he'd let go and smack me in the face a few times, then grab my head again.

I'd get so mad I'd burst into tears. Then Frank'd laugh like it was the funniest thing he ever seen.

One night I come home and Frank was standin' there ready to go at it.

"Can we please not do this tonight," I begged. "You're too rough, and I don't wanna fight with you."

Frank would make his voice sound like mine and say, "Can we please not do this tonight? Fine, you little brat. Bring me your books and let me see what homework you have."

I was shocked. Frank never let me off that easy. What was he up to? He never cared about my homework 'fore. I ran to get my reader and brought it back to Frank. He opened the reader and a slip of paper fell out. Oh no! I held my breath. I had forgotten about that note.

My mind went back to earlier that day when Mrs. Calhoun sent me to see Principal Brown.

"So, young man, Mrs. Calhoun tells me she has a joker in her class. Would you like to come over here and see how funny my paddle can be?"

"No, sir." I put my head down.

"Well, I want you to understand we do not tolerate foolishness in the classroom. I am giving you your last warning. If I catch you doin' anything else wrong, not only will you get a paddling, but you will also be suspended from school. Do you understand?"

I shook my head yes.

Then Mr. Brown scribbled somethin' on a piece of paper and said, "I want you to deliver this note to your parents so they can make sure this behavior does not happen again."

I didn't know how I was gonna explain the note so I tucked it in my reader and had forgot about it until then. Maybe Frank didn't see it fall to the floor. I got closer and put my foot on top of it.

T. S. Kincaid

"Move back, boy. Give me some space while I look at this here book. See Spot Run, Run, Spot, Run. He read it out loud. "What the hell kind of reader is this? This is like a baby book."

I sometimes have a hhhard time readin' so Mrs. Calhoun makes mmme practice with this."

I slid the piece of paper with my foot as I backed away.

"What the hell's wrong with you, why you actin' like that? You never ssssstuter   unless you done something. Now fess up."

"I ain't done nothin'" I lied.

'Well, don't just stand there, get me another beer."

I tried to scoot my foot along the floor when Frank said, "Well, well, well. What do we have here?"

He pushed me over and picked up the paper from the floor.

"Aww somebody's in trouble now. Says here we have a class clown on our hands and that you've been caught talkin' too much."

"No, I…"

"Don't you dare lie to me, boy!" Frank grabbed me by the shirt collar and pulled me close to his face. I could smell the beer on his breath.

I'M TIMMY

"I'm gonna give you one chance, when you go to that school tomorrow, you'd better not say one word, not one, you hear me?"

"Yes, sir."

"Now go get me that beer, and do your homework."

I couldn't believe I got off so easy.

I sat at the table and studied my spellin' words 'til Frank said it was time to eat.

"What is it?" I asked.

"How the hell should I know? It's somethin' your mama fixed 'fore she left for work."

I put my books away as Frank put the bowl on the table.

"Hey, tonight *Adventures of Superman* is on televison. You think maybe we could watch it together?" I asked.

"Maybe," Frank scooped out what was in the pot into the bowl.

I scrunched up my nose when I saw what it was. Vegetable soup. Eww. I hated vegetable soup more than anythin'. I don't even like the smell of it. I took a deep breath. I put my spoon in it and started stirrin' it 'round. I put some on the spoon and blew on it. Then I put it back in the bowl.

"Quit playin' with your food and eat." Frank said.

"I was wonderin' if I could have somethin' else. I don't like vegetable soup much.

"Well, too damn bad. This is what your mama fixed and you're gonna eat it."

I stirred it once again and picked it up and dumped it back in the bowl. Then I took my finger and thumb and pinched my nose. Frank smacked my hand away.

I put the spoon back in the bowl and got a big scoop. Then I put it in my mouth. I gagged. Before I knew what was happenin' I started throwin' up right in that there bowl of soup.

Frank jumped up. "Shit boy! You do that every damn time. Well, this time you're not gonna get away with it. You're gonna sit here and eat every last bite of that soup do you hear me?"

"But.."

My eyes started to blur and I wanted to say that usually mama just let's me throw it away. Before I could get all of that out, Frank grabbed the back of my head and put his arm up under my neck. "Open your damn mouth, boy."

He pinched my nose 'til I could no longer hold my breath. I gasped and when I did Frank shoved that soup, vomit and all right in my mouth.

I'M TIMMY

He took his hands and clamped my jaws together. Movin' 'em up and down. Vomit and soup sprayed through my nose. It burned and I felt like I was chokin'. I started gaspin' for air.

"Good God! You disgust me. Clean up this shit and get your ass in bed. You can go hungry tonight."

I cried and gagged the whole time I was wipin' that table and scootin' all that soup, snot, and vomit in the trash. My nose burned and my throat hurt. I couldn't keep my eyes and nose from runnin'.

"Hurry up and get your ass in the bed," Frank yelled.

"But… what about Superman?" I cried.

"Oh, you ruined your chances of any T.V. tonight, now finish cleanin' up that mess and get the hell out of my sight."

I ran to my room. I cried as I thought about how much I missed mama, I wished she'd come home. I worried 'bout what she would say about that note. I hated Frank, not just for what he'd done tonight, but for how mean he always is to mama. One of these days he wouldn't be as big and strong as he was now. And he would get his.

The next day I tried to remember what Frank said. I didn't say one word all day while I was in school. On the playground, was another story. Me and Jimmy and Tommy all ran around playin' tag and havin' fun. I liked playin' with them 'cause I was one of the fastest. I'd run up behind Tommy and yell, "Tag, you're it." When I got to the fence I coulda swore I seen our red and white car drivin' away.

That evenin' when I got home, soon as I walked in the door Frank told me to come and stand in front of him.

I did.

"Did you talk in school today, boy?" He asked.

"No sir, not in school." I said.

"Don't you lie to me, boy." His eyes looked like he didn't believe me.

"I'm not." I told him.

"I seen you, Timothy, so don't stand there and lie to me." His voice was gettin' loud.

I stood there and thought about it for a minute. Then I remembered.

"Oh, I didn't talk *in* school, but on the playgro...:

Next thing I knowed I was pickin' myself up off the floor, Both of the sides of my head hurt where Frank had hit me on one side and I hit the corner of the wall on the other.

"Get up!" He yelled.

I'M TIMMY

He grabbed me by the hair of my head and dragged me into the closet. He slammed the door. It was dark and I was hurtin' and scared.

"Please let me out, I promise I'll be good," I begged. I musta asked him a thousand times. Alls I could hear was the blastin' of the T.V. and Frank laughin' at the show he was watchin'.

That evenin' long after suppertime, mama came home. Right before she got there Frank opened the closet door and let me out. He placed his finger in front of his lips and said, "Shhhh," as he shook his head. Both my eyes was swollen and not just from cryin'.

When mama came in she asked me, "How'd you get them black eyes?"

I looked over at Frank who said, "He was fightin' in school."

"Fightin'?" Mama said. "Boy, you know I don't allow that. Go get my paddle."

Mama spanked me good for that. Now who's the liar?

Chapter 12

THE CLOCK WAS goin' tick, tick, tick on the wall each time the second hand moved. That was all I could hear sittin' in my seat waitin' for Mrs. Calhoun to give out the next spellin' word. She liked for the room to be real quiet when we was havin' a test. Sos people can concentrate, she'd said.

"APPRECIATE,' Mrs. Calhoun's voice cut through the silence. She walked around the room between the rows of seats. She stopped at mine. "I hope you APPRECIATE your Christmas gifts, APPRECIATE."

I stared at my paper. Just four more words to go. I closed my eyes and I tried to see the word in my head.

App- app, I was sure I knew it. Let's see. I kept my eyes closed and I started movin' my lips. I thought I was whisperin, but I must whisper like my Aunt Erma and kinda half whisper half mumble instead.

"Timothy!" Mrs. Calhoun startled me when she reached down and grabbed the spellin' paper off my desk. "No cheating, now go to your corner!"

"But, I wasn't cheat…"

"I said go to your corner. You know the consequences for cheating. That will be an automatic F, now go"

She pointed her long skinny finger toward the corner of the room that I'd been put in so many times; it was known as 'My Corner.'

I felt my face get all hot. My eyes filled with tears and one ran down my cheek before I could catch it. I wiped it away as fast as I could. Mrs. Calhoun looked down at my spellin' test and crumpled it up into a little ball.

"You were going to fail anyway," she said as she tossed it into the trash.

T. S. Kincaid

Everyone giggled.

"Quiet! Everyone, keep your eyes on your own paper. Timothy, I'm waiting."

I got up real slow from my desk and I walked as quiet as I could over to my corner. I stood facin' the gray cinderblock walls. I leaned over ever so slightly sos not to get any attention and peeked out the winda. I seen a snowflake fall.

I wanted to say, "Look everyone! It's snowin'."

But I decided to keep that secret to myself. My wish for a Christmas snow was comin' true. Maybe Santa would come with a nice shiny new sled for me. Even though Frank told me there ain't no Santa, and he wouldn't be bringin' me nothin' even if there was. That didn't stop me from wishin' and hopin' I'd get me a new sled anyways.

I peeked out again, and this time the snow was really comin' down. It looked so pretty with it's big giant snowflakes swirlin' round and fallin' softly to the ground. I 'magined little snow fairies glidin' round, dancin' on the wind.

"Look!" Tommy Tucker pointed to the winda. "It's snowin'!"

He had blabbed my private happiness to the whole class, and now my secret was out.

I'm Timmy

All the kids came runnin' to look out at the beautiful snowfall.

"Now, children, settle down. Everyone go back to your seats."

All the kids kept talkin' as they walked back to their seats and sat down.

"Timothy?" Do you have wax in your ears?"

All the kids laughed.

"No ma'am," I said. I could feel my face getting' hot again.

"Well, make sure, because you are NOT listening. I said everyone back to your seats."

"Yes ma'am." I said.

I slowly made my way back to my seat and sat down. I'd heard her, but how was I supposed to know she was talkin' to me? One minute she was tellin' me to get in the corner, and the next she was tellin' me to get out. That was the shortest time I ever spent in that corner. She never talks to me, 'cept to tell me what I'm doin' wrong.

"Now, children, I know you are excited about the snow and this being the last day before Christmas break, but if you promise to be really good and keep your voices down, I'll now give out the gifts."

All of the kids quietly said they promised.

"When I call your name, you may quietly come up to the front and claim your present."

I was so excited. I'd never done anything like this at my other school. Mrs. Calhoun sat in her chair beside the Christmas tree. She started callin' out the names and one by one each kid went up to get their gift. I was about to bust. I sat as quiet as I could to listen for my name.

The lights on the tree were all shiny. . They were all different colors. I could see all the drums, and balls and tinsel movin' just a little bit in the draft. We'd all been told to each bring an ornament from home to put on the tree. We ain't got a tree. I begged mama and Frank to go to the tree farm, I'd heard tell about. The other kids said they was horse- drawn wagons, and you could actually go and pick out your own tree right there on the spot. They'd even cut it down for ya. They even said there was hot chocolate, and a big ole light display. Man, that was surely somethin' I'd love to see.

"Please, please, please can we go?" I'd even got down on my knees and put my hands up like I's prayin' as I begged.

"Are you stupid, or what?" Frank looked at me like I was some kinda dummy. "We ain't got enough gas money to take your mama to work, much less go to some damn tree farm."

"Well, we might if somebody would get off his lazy ass and get a job!" Mama blurted out.

"Bitch! You know I'm on suspension!" Then the fightin' would start.

Since I didn't have no Christmas tree, I didn't have no ornaments to bring to school. Then I got me an idea. I'd just make one. I went around the house and gathered up all the pretty paper I could find. I carefully folded and cut it as best I could to make a beautiful star. When I showed it to mama, she didn't say much. But I thought it was pretty. I could just see the look on Mrs. Calhoun's face now. She'd be so surprised. Well, she might even be nice to me and let me put that star on the very top of our class Christmas tree.

But, as always, things didn't turn out the way I thought they was gonna. When I got to school on that cold day, I pulled that star out from where I had it tucked inside my coat. I was so proud when I held it up to show it to Mrs. Calhoun. I couldn't help but have the biggest grin on my face.

"What's that stupid thing?" Tommy Tucker blurted out. The whole class laughed. I was so ashamed I wanted to throw it in the trash and run out the door and never come back. But I didn't. I just stood there lookin' like a dummy.

"Well? What is it?" Mrs. Calhoun asked. She had her nose scrunched up like I did whenever someone gives me vegetable soup.

"It's a star for the tree," I whispered.

"Oh, I see." Said Mrs. Calhoun she took it from my hands with her thumb and finger and held it like it had cooties or somethin'.

"That's the ugliest thing I ever seen." Said Bobbie Sue.

The class roared again.

"Well, what did you expect?" said Mrs. Calhoun, "The sad part is he probably really tried."

She took my star and tucked it way up under the tree. I had to look real hard before I finally seen it way in the back.

"Well class, that's all. You may take your gifts home with you and put them under your own tree. Now remember, don't open them until Christmas."

I'M TIMMY

I sat there with my brows together. Then I slowly raised my hand.

"Now, children, there is one more thing that I would like for us to do." She opened her bottom desk drawer and pulled out a small birthday cake. "Now, I know we have all talked about and are all excited about Santa coming, but I want you to know the real reason for the Christmas season. Can anyone tell me?"

Every hand went up.

"What is it, Timothy?"

"You didn't call my name," I said.

"What? Are you sure? Oh! That's right; now I remember. I said everyone would get a gift if they didn't have any absences. Remember? Of course you don't because you weren't here."

"But Bobbie Sue got a gift and she weren't here." I argued.

"Wasn't here," Mrs. Calhoun huffed. "Bobbie Sue had chicken pox and couldn't help being absent. Now, did you have chicken pox?"

"No, but.."

"That's what I thought. Now oversleeping and missing your bus is not an excuse."

I wanted so bad to explain. I had good reason for missin' my bus. And it wasn't just oversleepin'. Mama

167

and Frank had a big night out on the town, and they come in staggerin' drunk. Frank passed out on the couch, while I spent the rest of the night holdin' Mama's hair back and gettin' her a wet warsh rag, while she puked her guts out in the toilet. They both had hangovers the next day and slept in. They forgot to wake me. Mama made me swear not to ever tell a livin' soul and I never did.

"Now, there will be no more arguing about it. Understand?" I was told by Mrs. Calhoun.

"Now getting back to what I was saying, the reason we celebrate Christmas is that it is for the Baby Jesus' birthday."

She pulled a tall white candle from her top drawer and placed it on the cake.

"You all did very well on your spelling test. Well, except one, but anyway, only one of you made one hundred percent. Sally? Would you come up here, please?"

It made me sick how Sally rushed up to Mrs. Calhoun's desk. Like she was some kinda teacher's pet or somethin'.

"Now class, we are all going to sing Happy Birthday, and Sally, you may make a wish and blow out the candle."

Sally's bucktoothed smile turned my stomach.

I put my head down on my desk.

"Now, everyone stand as we sing Happy Birthday."
I didn't budge.

"Anyone not standing, will not get a piece of birthday cake."

I kept my head down. I didn't care about singin' or eatin' any dumb birthday cake. I just wanted this day to be over.

"Suit yourself," Mrs. Calhoun said, and she led the class in song.

Sally made her stupid wish and blew out the candle.

Finally, the day was over.

"Class, remember, there will be no school for the next two weeks. I hope ya'll have a Merry Christmas. Class dismissed."

The class all lined up in a hurry. Each one was tryin' to cut in front of the other one, when we all raced through the hall to the outside bus loading area.

"Order!" Shouted Mrs. Calhoun, "We must have order! Now, everyone, come back and start again."

T. S. Kincaid

We all groaned and went back down the hallway and lined up again. We went single file all the way back down the hall and out into the school bus loading area. I shivered and tried to keep my balance on the slippery sidewalk.

Mrs. Calhoun stood rockin' back and forth rubbin' her the arms of her coat with her gloved hands. She kept lookin' at her watch and then she'd search for the bus and look at her watch again.

It was cold.

I stood there shiverin', My hands was freezin'. Oh no! I forgot one of my mittens. Mama and Frank was gonna kill me.

I ran up to Mrs. Calhoun and I said, "Mrs. Calhoun, may I please go back into the classroom? I forgot one of my mittens."

"No! You had your chance to get all of your things when you were dismissed. Now get in line."

"But Ma'am, you don't understand. I will get in a lot of trouble if I don't have that mitten. Please?"

Mrs. Calhoun looked at me. For the very first time her face seemed to soften, and she sighed. She looked around.

"Susan, come here," she ordered one of the older girls from one of the other classes.

I'm Timmy

"Yes, Mrs. Calhoun?"

"Listen, they say we have a huge storm coming in. I thought that it would hold off until later, but it doesn't look like it. I have a very important doctor's appointment I need to get to. I'd like to try and beat this weather before it gets any worse. If I leave now, will you make sure that everyone gets on that bus?"

"Are you going to find out if you are going to have a baby? I heard you and Mother talking the other night." Susan said with a wide smile.

"Yes, yes, hopefully, that will be Mr. Calhoun's Christmas present. Now, will you do that for me? I have to go, not a word to anyone."

"Sure thing, not a problem, Mrs. Calhoun," Susan promised.

Mrs. Calhoun waved me on saying, "Okay, Timothy, but be quick about it."

I raced back into the empty school buildin'. It was kinda creepy how quiet it was. My wet shoes made a chirping sound on that shiny floor as I ran down that long hallway.

When I got to my classroom I started lookin' for my mitten. I know it's here somewhere. Darn, not in my desk. Maybe it's under it. I got down on my hands and knees 'til my ear was almost touchin the floor. I could smell that thick wax. I looked not only under my desk but everyone else's too.

Nothin' but dust.

Maybe the cloakroom. I ran to where we hung up our coats, but it weren't there either. Oh man, where is it? I looked through each cubby and then looked again. It's no use. I'm gonna have to take my beatin'. Then I glanced up and I seen it hangin' over the top shelf just out of my reach. Now how did that get up there? I jumped over and over 'til finally, I managed to grab the tip of it. But it slipped. Damn. Then I jumped one more time and shew, I got it.

I ran back to the door and I was just steppin' into the hall, when I heared footsteps and somebody whistlin'. The sound was echoin' off the empty hall walls. It was Mr. Brown. I froze. I knowed if he caught me in here I was gonna be suspended for sure. He was comin' closer and closer down the hall. What am I gonna do? Hide, I told myself. I tiptoed as fast as I could back to the cloakroom. I hid behind the only coat that was hangin' there. My heart started poundin' as I stood there.

He was at the next classroom over. I could hear his footsteps gettin' louder and louder. Oh, why don't he just come on. I thought he was gonna pass by, but no! He came in the classroom. I held my breath, but my heart was still beatin' so loud I knowed he could hear it.

He started walkin' round the room. What is he doin'?

Finally, he went back out, shut the door and walked on down the hall. I should go. No, I decided to wait just a few more minutes. What if he comes back? I could still hear him walkin and whistlin'. I would wait til I couldn't hear that no more.

When I was for sure he was gone, I decided to make my move. I got to the door and put my ear against it. I heard a big bang and I reckon that was the outside door he went out of. I turned the door knob, but nothin' happened. I turned it again, and this time I pressed on the door. Still nothing'. My hands started shakin' and I was shakin' it real hard when I figured out the door was locked.

No, no, no, no, no!

I ran to the winda and looked out. It was pourin the snow. I couldn't hardly see nothin' but white. Then I seen back car lights. You know, the red ones. It must have been Mr. Brown's truck leavin'.

But wait, Susan would know that I'm missin and she'll tell somebody. Course she will. I waited and listened. Alls I could hear was the howlin' wind. I couldn't hear no buses or nothin' else.

The words Mrs. Calhoun said kept runnin through my head. "Class, we will be out for two weeks." Two weeks, I didn't know much about time yet, but I knowed two weeks was almost like a million years.

I ran back over to the winda. It started rattlin'. That was scary. Maybe if I opened it I could yell for somebody to help me. I tried to push it open, but it was stuck. Think, think, think. There had to be some thin' I could do.

I started bangin' and yellin' and screamin' as loud as I could. I was jumpin'up and down and yellin' my head off. I looked out the winda again. Alls I could see was the side walk. The wind was blowin; the snow all around. I looked up and in the buildin' across from me. I couldn't believe it. There was a boy in the winda. I waved. He waved.

Hey! I started waving 'both hands and jumpin' up and down. So did he. He must be stuck in the other buildin' just like me. Just like me. Just. Like. me. I noticed he did everythin' I did. I stood there and screamed. It was me.

How could I be so stupid?

I'm Timmy

I started screamin' and yellin."' Somebody! Anybody! Help me!"

Wait, was that a truck engine I heard? I ran to the far winda but couldn't quite see. I dragged Mrs. Calhoun's heavy wooden chair as close as I could. I stood on tiptoes and pressed my face against the cold winda pane.

Hey! HHHHEEYY!. I yelled so loud my throat hurt. And my fists was achin' from poundin' on the winda so hard.

I jumped from the chair and grabbed the paperweight on top of Mrs. Calhoun's desk. I threw it at the winda as hard as I could. Glass came rainin' down bein' blown back in by that wicked wind. I ran to the winda again, and stretched my neck real far. I thought I saw a man scrapin' the snow off his car. I hollored, but the wind caught my words and threw them away.

I squinted my eyes as the snow covered my lashes. I yelled so long and so hard that my voice couldn't hardly make any sounds. My throat was so dry. And I was so very, very cold. I went back to my desk and laid my head down. The air swooped in and stole what little heat I had. I ran back to the cloakroom and I found that other coat. I shivered as I pulled my knees to my chest and I could see thick smoke comin' out of my mouth each time I took a breath. My teeth were chatterin' so loud, it was makin' my jaws cramp.

Surely the buses were near my home by now. When Frank figured out that I didn't get off the bus, he'd come for me. He'd be real pissed off, but he'd come.

Just wait.

But I was so cold. Colder than I've ever been. Even colder than that time Frank made me sit in that ice cold water til mama came home. She kept askin' me why my lips was so blue. I bet they was really blue now.

It was startin' to get dark outside. The buildin' was getting' dark too. Before too long I wouldn't be able to see nothin' at all. I tried to cover the hole in the winda but the wind just kept uncoverin it.

Frank will be here any minute now. I just know it. Seems like it's gettin' darker by the second.

Oh! I'm so cold.

I tried to get in the corner of the cloakroom but that didn't help. The wind was swirlin' 'round all through the room.

Oh! I am so, so cold. If I only had some heat. Somethin', anything.

I'M TIMMY

Then I remembered the candle. Mrs. Calhoun had lit a candle. If I could just find that candle and some matches, I could light me a fire.

Now where did she put it? I wasn't payin' any attention when they was singin' that stupid birthday song. I slowly made my way back to her desk. My arms and legs was stiff and I felt like my blood was freezin'.

Oh my, how it hurt!

My hands was shakin' so bad, I couldn't open the drawers. Damn! Where was that candle? I finally pulled the middle drawer out and there it was. It rolled to the edge. A smile coulda froze on my face and I wouldn't a cared. Now I needed the matches. I felt around for them, but they weren't there. I bbbbettt that ddddamn bbbbitch put 'em in her ppppocket. I said right out loud. I hopelessly hunted.

Oh wait! I remembered. That top far shelf. Whew! There they was. I could hardly close my fingers around the small box. I made it to the center of the room and put the candle on the floor. It took a while, but I got that match box open. The box rattled in my hand and some of the matches spilled out on the floor. My hands were killin' me. I shoved them up in my jacket and I rubbed and rubbed them 'til they stopped stingin' so bad.

T. S. Kincaid

I struck the match.

The fire came to life, then whoosh it went out.

I tried again and again. I was so tired and cold, alls I wanted to do was lay down.

No! I'm not gonna lay down. Think! But I can't think. It's too cold to think. I fell over on the floor and hit the metal trashcan. That's it. I put the candle and the matches in the trashcan and made my way to the far corner.

I hunched over the can tryin' my best to keep the wind away. I put my hands down in the can and lit the match. As fast as I could I grabbed the candle and it lit. Woo hoo! That little light glowing inside of that trash can was the prettiest thing I ever seen, 'sides Mama. I moved my hand back and forth over the flame.

Oh no! What if it goes out? The thought scared me to death. I had to find some way to keep the fire goin'. What could I use? Paper! I seen some paper in the desks. I went as fast as I could an grabbed as many pieces as I could find. The paper burned fast and lit up the room a little more sos I could see. It's gonna go out soon. I need more. Somethin' with a lot of paper. Books! That's it. We got lots of books. I scooted over to the bookshelf and found the biggest books I could find. I carefully put them on top of the burnin' paper. Real gentle like, sos not to smother the flame.

The fire grew. My numb hands started to tingle like a thousand needles was stabbin' em. I was just startin' to warm up, when I got me another idea.

Maybe if the fire was bigger, someone would see it and they would know that I was here. I put my mittens back on and dragged the flamin' can back across the wood floor and put it near the winda. It was colder here, but at least somebody would be able to see the light.

I started laughin' so hard. I piled those books on top of each other. It was really getting tall. Surely someone would see it. Wonder what Frank will say when he finds out I burned up all them books? I know he'll be real mad 'cause I bet the school will make him pay for every one of 'em. I know what he'll say. He's gonna take it outta my hide, that's what he'll say.

Yessir, I bet I get a beatin' for every dollar he and mama'll have to spend. But you know what? I bet no matter how mad Frank and mama are gonna be, they might, just maybe, be kind of proud of me for thinkin' of startin' the fire in the first place.

It started to warm up now. And the warmer I got, I got to dancin' 'round. I went 'round the room and found even more books. Oh Wow! Would you look at that? It's the biggest book I ever seen. If I could just put this one on the fire, it will surely burn 'til they get here. I picked that book up real high in the air and tossed it down into that trash can. But you know what? That can tipped over and a gust of wind swirled around and picked up all that soot and hot ashes. Soon as that fire hit that wax on that wood floor, the room roared to life. I gasped. That fire spread like lightnin'speed through that room. I ran all around beatin' at those flames. But the more I tried to put it out the bigger it got.

Now black smoke and fire swirled and danced from one spot to the next. I was shocked at how fast it was runnin up the walls and up to the ceilin'. I put my shirt over my face and ran to the door. I banged and banged on that door.

Mama? I screamed. Mama! Where are you? Mama please!! I cried. The smoke stung my eyes and burned my insides. I ran to the opened winda. But the wind just made it worse.

Where is Frank? Why isn't anybody comin? Don't they see the schools on fire? Pieces of burnin' ceilin' started to fall. Some hit me on my arms and legs. My clothes were on fire.

I'M TIMMY

Mama! Mama! I screamed. The pain was unbearable. The more I ran, the worse it got. The fire was all over me now. Burnin' my skin, and I felt like I was bein' cooked alive.

A huge burnin' beam creaked and moaned as it fell from the ceilin'. It hit me right on the top of my head. I crashed to the floor just as it gave way beneath me. I was fallin' with all those burin' timbers to the bottomless pit…

Chapter 13

THE SUN WAS so bright and the morning sky was my favorite of the bluest blue. The far away voices got louder. Men were moving around, digging and scraping. Steam was coming up from all of the mess on the ground. I walked around as they passed out coffee and picked up their tools. They finally all climbed into the fire trucks and went on their way. I saw two men standing, talking. Sos I decided to go up to them.

I'M TIMMY

"Yes, it's a shame. From the looks of it, it's a total loss. Damn thing must have burnt all night. Hitting that coal furnace musta been what caused the explosion. Thank God no one was here. Brown said he was the last to leave last evenin'. The fire must have started sometime after he left."

The fire? Oh yes, now I remember, the fire. I stood looking around at all of the snow and busted glass and brick that lay everywhere. The sun shining on the snow looked like thousands of sparkling diamonds. Funny, even though it was so bright, I didn't even squint my eyes. The sunshine didn't bother me. Nothing seemed to bother me. I didn't feel no cold, I wasn't hungry, or nervous, or tired. I made my way over to where the men were with ease.

"Wonder how it started?" Said one of the men.

"I started it." I thought it'd be best to go ahead and tell the truth right away sos I could deal with the consequences.

"I'm sorry, but I lit the fire because it was so awfully cold, and I wanted to get somebody's attention."

"Who knows?" said the man in the yellow fire hat. "Could'a been faulty wirin' or anythin'. If it hadn't been for that storm, I'd a said it was damn vandals. No one in his right mind woulda been out on a night like that. Hell, our fire trucks wouldn't a been able to get up this knoll, even if we'd wanted to. No one even knew the damn thing was on fire 'til it blew up. The investigator will be here tomorrow. This is a mess. It's gonna take weeks, if not months to sort this out. But I say we'll probably never know."

What was wrong with them? Didn't they hear me? I moved a little closer.

"Excuse me, It was me who set the fire. Can someone please take me home?" I asked.

"Alright then. Tell the investigator to get me his report as soon as he can. We've got an emergency board meetin' Tuesday. We'll have to figure out what we're gonna do. Shit! It's cold!" The man was shivering as he put his hand out to shake the other man's hand.

The other man told him, "Will do."

They both turned and had a hard time getting through the slushy snow, slipping and sliding all the way back to their trucks. I tagged along. Both of the men got in their trucks and started their engines. I stood waiting to see which one would open the door for me since I weren't sure who I'd be ridin' with. Can you believe they both backed out one right after the other and drove away?

I'M TIMMY

I stood there, not believing those men just left me there like that. Maybe they was mad 'cause the fire was my fault. Still, you'd a thought they'd a said something.

"They couldn't hear you, bubby."

Who said that? That sounded like Daddy. I turned around and could't believe it.

"Daddy? Is that you?" I still couldn't believe it. "What are you doing here?"

"I've come to get you. You have to come with me now, son. There ain't much time."

"Have you come to take me home?" I smiled the widest smile. "Oh boy, I can't wait to see the look on Frank's face. And mama. Mama will be so happy."

"Not exactly. Just come on. We have to hurry." Daddy put his hand out for me.

"But I want my Mama," I told him.

"You can't Timmy.You don't understand, bubby. You have to come with me or you'll miss your chance. I'm not even supposed to be here and neither are you. I can't force you. It has to be your decision, but I'm asking you to come with me now."

"I don't want to go," I told him. "I'm going home to see my Mama."

"Timothy, this is your last chance." Daddy looked at me with that special look of his when he meant business. "If you don't come with me right now, you will be stuck here for eternity. Eternity bubby, that's a long, long, time."

"Wait, what? Are you saying I'm... dead? That's not possible. How can I be dead if I am here talkin' to you? No, no. I don't believe you! I can't be dead. I'm only eight years old. I have my whole life to live."

"You have the rest of eternity now, son. Come on, we have to go. We can talk about all of this later."

"Later, when? And go where? I told you; I'm going home to Mama."

"Please, bubby,"

"Wait, you said it was my choice? Then, was it your choice? You mean you could've stayed with us, but instead, you decided to leave me and mama?"

I could feel my insides startin' to boil.

"It's not like that, bubby. I knew if I left you for what seemed to be a short time then, that you would be joining me soon enough, and we could all be together for all of eternity."

Hum, I thought to myself. I weren't so sure if I believed him, but he'd never lied to me before.

"Come on, son."

"No!" For the first time ever, I talked back to Daddy. "I am not leaving my mama. She needs me."

"Oh, Timmy." Daddy had the saddest look on his face; then, before I knowed it, he was gone.

"Daddy?"

I stood there real quiet for a minute. Feeling empty. Trying to get it in my head all that's happened. I'm dead. Really, truly, dead. But what does that mean? I feel alive. No, better than alive. It's as if all of my senses woke up. I can see, hear, smell, touch? I ran to the snow. I picked up some snow. I found I could move it around and make it do things, like squeeze into a ball, but couldn't feel it's cold. I put it to my tongue. Nothing. Great! The one sense I don't have, taste, was the one I'd miss the most. So, I'm dead. But for some reason, I feel different. More aware. Wiser, like I understand things better than before.

I thought of mama. Like a snap of a finger, I was with her. Right by her side in the diner. Mama looked tired. She was standing by the coffee pot, pouring herself a cup. I knew she was surely going to be surprised to see me.

"Hi, Mama."

She didn't look up. She just kept right on drinking her coffee. "Mama, are you mad at me? I'm so sorry about the school, but it was so cold and that was the only thing I could think to do."

Mama just sat there, starin' straight ahead. Wait a minute. What was she doing here at work anyways? Don't she know I didn't come home last night? Weren't she worried?

Mama picked up the phone, tapped on the receiver and waited. She finally put it back down.

"Still dead." She told the man in the kitchen. "You really think we're gonna get any customers in this weather? I bet theys two feet of snow, if not more out there."

"Oh, I suppose you're right, Lou Ann. I thought people might need to come here to get a bite to eat if they were out of power. But seeing as the main road's been clear for nearly an hour, and no one's been in here, we might as well close up shop. Thanks a lot for stayin' last night."

"Oh, I didn't mind, better than Frank comin' out in that storm.

A man came into the diner. He looked at mama's boss and said did you hear about the explosion over in Frankfort? Someone said it was the elementary school.

"Oh God! I hope nobody got hurt." Said Mama.

"Nah, they said it was last night after dark and all the buses had run."

"Well, that's good. Now, what are they gonna do when it's time for the kids to go back after break?" Mama asked.

"Don't know. Said they's havin' a meetin' on Tuesday to decide."

"Want a cup of coffee?" asked Mama.

The man said no and that he was just comin' in to tell her boss the news.

Mama looked at her boss and said, "I still can't get ahold of Frank. You think maybe you could give me a lift?"

"I'd be glad to." He told her.

So that's why mama didn't know I didn't come home last night. Of course. She wouldn't be at work if she did. But why didn't Frank call her to let her know? Oh, yeah, Mama said the phone weren't working.

After they closed up the diner, we got in her bosses car, and he took us all the way to the end of our road. Mama thanked him when she got out and almost closed the door on me. I decided to stay with her and see what Frank had to say when she got home.

Mama tromped through that snow like a champ. She slipped once, but I caught her by the arm and steadied her. You should have seen the look on her face. She jumped like she'd seen a ghost, but as far as I could tell, she couldn't see me. At least she doesn't act like it if she can.

There was no car in the driveway, and when we got in the house there was no Frank.

"Frank?" Mama yelled. "Hey, you here?' Huh, wonder where he could be? Timothy?

"Yes, Mama," I said, surprised; maybe she could see me after all.

"Timothy? You home? Now I wonder where the hell those two are. Oh, shit. I hope they didn't go to get me. Now Frank's gonna really be pissedl"

I guess she was talking to herself.

She went over and picked up the phone and banged on the receiver to see if anybody answered. No one picked up. She slammed the phone down. "Damn, the lines must still be down." She said out loud again.

Funny how we never had a phone until we moved in with Frank. Lots of our neighbors were mad because they said mama and Frank were always hogging the line.

Mama said she would be so glad the day they could do away with party lines. She said she never had any privacy, because she could always hear someone else picking up the line and listening in on her conversations.

Someone calls all hours of the night but never talks when mama answers. Mama asked the operator who it was, but all the operator would say was that it was coming from a private party.

I tried to use the phone to call my Mawmaw Pike once, but Frank told me to keep my grubby little hands off of it and said if he ever caught me trying to use it again, he'd break my fingers.

I thought being with mama was wonderful. I know that I am dead, but now I can spend all of my time with mama. Even if she couldn't see me, I could always be with her and watch over her.

She went into the bathroom and turned on the water for the tub. I decided to go see what Frank was up to.

Instantly, I was sitting beside Frank in Mama's car at Ollies Texaco. He was talking to the attendant about the fire.

"Sure as hell, musta been some blast." Frank said. He shivered. Then he turned the heat up in the car. "Damn, it's so cold."

"That'll be three dollars and sixteen cents." Said the attendant.

"No, problem." Frank reached into his wallet and pulled out a five-dollar bill. He looked over and honked the horn. The same lady that I had seen at our house before came over to his window.

"Hey baby, where you been? I've been tryin' to call you." The lady said.

"Oh, I've been around. Where you goin'?" Frank asked her.

"Oh, I'm just about to take Judy home. She isn't feelin' well. That time of the month ya know?."

"Oh, okay. Do you think you'll be able to get away later?" Frank asked.

"I don't know. Steve's been actin' awful suspicious lately. He even insists on drivin' me to work in the squad car. We better lay low for a while."

"Whatever you say, baby." Frank grabbed her necklace and rubbed his hand down her sweater, touching her breast.

Looking around, she grabbed his hand and said, "Oh, you're bad. See ya."

The woman walked back to her car. There was a teenage girl in the passenger side. I heard her say, "Hey Mother, wasn't that Frank Walker?"

I'M TIMMY

I didn't pay any attention to what the mother said. I was too busy wondering what Frank was going to do next. He headed home.

When we got back to the house Mama was laying in her bed. Frank came in and said, "Well, it's about time you got your ass home."

"What's that supposed to mean? Where the hell have you been?" Mama asked.

"Where do you think? I went to the diner to pick up your ass."

"That's a lie Mama," I said.

"How'd you get home anyways?" Frank asked

"Al gave me a ride."

"Oh, you mean your boyfriend? What are you screwin' him now?' Frank sneered.

"Shut up. Don't be stupid. You know he's just my boss." Replied mama.

"Hey woman, watch your mouth. Get up and fix me somethin' to eat. I ain't ate all day."

"Well, what have you been doin' all day? Here rub my feet, they're awful tired."

"Yeah, I bet. Where exactly did you sleep anyways?"

"On the little cot in the back of the diner. I told you I was stayin'. That storm was really something last night. And did you hear about the school?"

"Yeah, yeah, hurry up, I'm starved."

Mama got up to fix Frank a sandwich. She looked out the window. "Tell Tim to come on in. He can eat too."

"Tim? I ain't seen that little shit all day."

"What do you mean? Wasn't he with you?"

"Hell no, I got up this mornin' and checked his room, he was gone and out the door 'fore I got to see him."

"That's another lie, Mama."

"You mean he's been out in this cold all day?" Mama went to the door. "Timothy! Get your ass in here now." She yelled. "Alls I need is a doctor bill for that little bastard."

Mama finished making Frank's sandwich, then she made mine and sat it on the table.

"Don't you think it's cold in here?" She said as she walked over and turned up the gas.

"Hell, I've been chillin' all day. I may have to get that heat checked in the car. Damn thing stayed cold all the way home."

I'M TIMMY

Mama told Frank she was tired and that she was going to lie down for a while. He told her he would join her and they both went into the bedroom together. I decided to sit and wait. After a while that got awful boring, sos I decided to go down to the local park and hang out for a while.

For the first time I didn't have to ask nobody, I could just go on my own. When I got to the park, I was surprised to see a girl there swinging on the swings. I thought I'd be alone, with it being so cold and all. I got closer.

"Well, lawd, look at choo. You look like you been run through the ringer. What happened?"

"You can see me?" I was in shock.

"Course I can. I ain't been hangin' round for the past ninety-three years for nothin', you know."

"Ninety -three years? Wow!!!"

"Yep, ninety-three years, seven months, thirteen hours, eleven minutes, and thirty-nine seconds to be exact. Are ya gonna tell me what happened or not?"

I stood there thinking, finally, I said, "I was in a fire."

"Well, I can see that. How'd it happen?"

I was too embarrassed to tell her all about it.

She started laughing right out loud. "You big dummy. All over a silly mitten?"

"Wait. How did you know that?"

"Why, I read your mind, of course. Show me what you looked like before."

I didn't know what she meant.

"I mean before you died."

"How can I do that?" I asked.

"Oh, Lawd, you greenhorns don't know nothin'. Look here, alls ya gotta do is concentrate real hard on the way you looked before. You don't wanna go around looking like that all the time, now do you?"

I didn't know. I weren't sure what I looked like.

"Well, it ain't very pretty," she said, after readin' my mind again.

"Will you stop doin' that? Sides boys ain't supposed to look pretty."

"Just do it. Now concentrate. Harder… harder."

I looked down and saw my hands and arms forming. Then my whole body was intact and I was my old self again.

"Oh, well, you ain't so bad to look at now." The girl said.

"Thanks, I think."

I'M TIMMY

I looked at her long braids and frumpy dress that came down to her knees. She had on thick stockings and shoes that buttoned all the way up her ankles.

"So, I'm guessing this is the way you looked before?" I asked.

"You mean, before I was shot?" She turned and showed me the back of her bloodied head; when she turned back around, there was a big ole hole in her face, and her left eye was missing.

I gasped.

"Great effect, huh? I only do that when I'm wantin' to scare somebody." She smiled as she changed back into the girl I had seen before.

"Why would you want to do that?" I asked.

"Oh, you'd be surprised. You gotta name?"

"Timmy."

"I'm Klara."

Klara and I talked the rest of the afternoon. I found out she stayed for her Mama, too.

She'd been walkin' across a field goin' to take water to her papa who was one of the wounded soldiers. When she finally found him, she saw that he was dead. He'd been dead for a while 'cause his body was all stiff. She stood to run back to the house when that stray bullet hit her. She knew she was the only thing her mama had left and couldn't bear to leave her.

"This here was our farm, 'fore the war. Our house used to sit right over yonder. And see that big oak tree? That's where my papa built me the finest rope swing you ever seen. Swingin' was my favorite thing to do."

"I like it, too." I said.

"I sure scared the bejesus outta them fellers who come to cut it down one day. They ain't been back since. Both me and mama are buried right under that big branch there."

"Buried?" I hadn't thought about that. Mama would have no body to bury seeing as how I got blown up.

"Hey, how come I'm not in little tiny pieces, I mean since the school exploded and all?" I asked.

"We look like we looked at the time of our death, not what happens to our bodies afterwards."

"Oh." I said. That made sense.

I wondered if mama would have wanted to take my body back to be buried beside Daddy.

"Hey, will you stop thinkin' about our shells?"

"Shells?" I asked.

I'm Timmy

"Our bodies. Don't you know by now that they's just a shell and we ain't even in 'em no more? So, what does it matter what happens to 'em?"

I thought for a second. Maybe it mattered to some people.

"Only livin' people," said Klara.

"Will you please stop readin' my mind? It bothers me." I told her.

"I can't help it. It is just a habit."

I guess she heard me think *well, I don't like it,* 'cause she said, "Okay, I'll try."

"Okay. Hey, do you think we could practice my showin' and not showin' myself?"

I already knowed I could travel on my thoughts. I figured that out on my own 'cause each time I thought of someone or something, I was instantly there. It was this showing myself or not showing myself, I was having trouble with.

"I reckon." She sighed. "It's like I said, alls ya gotta do is think about it. And concentrate."

I thought as hard as I could.

"Well, put your tongue back in your mouth," Klara said.

"Sorry, I do that when I'm concentratin'. My daddy used to do the same thing. Like when he'd be showin' me how to do somethin' and…"

"Will you focus?" Klara shouted. "Sometimes, you ain't got to show yourself atall, lots of us do that."

"What do you mean?"

"Well, it's like when I come down here to swing on my swing. I don't want a lot of people going into hysterics, so, I just don't show myself at all. I let 'em make themselves believe that the swing is movin' cause of the wind, instead of the real reason, which is I'm sittin' in it"

"Oh, yeah." I was startin' to understand things a lot better.

Before too long, I had it. I could show my livin' self, my dead self, and become invisible. I liked being invisible most of all. Just think of all the places I could go. I thought about the beach, and 'fore I knowed it, I was there. Wow! I was amazed at how big the ocean was.

"Come on back now," I heard Klara in my head. "I got some things to do."

"No, you don't; you just want shed of me," I said as I came back to her side.

I'M TIMMY

"Now who's readin' minds?" she smiled. I liked her smile. It was soft and friendly.

"Klara, before you go, there's just one more thing. I don't even think my Mama knows I'm dead yet."

This really bothered me.

"Then, you need to tell her." Klara said.

"I don't think she can hear me. I tried talkin' to her, but she didn't act like I was there. I don't want to scare her."

"Well, they's two ways you can go about it, unlessen they're close to death, then they see you anyways." Klara explained.

Number one, you can get real angry and yell at 'em, or number two, you can go to 'em while they're sleepin'. Usually, after that, they can hear you real good. It's the same as appearin' in front of 'em. Either be real good and mad or you gotta concentrate real hard."

It was getting late, and I decided I'd better get back to mama. I asked Klara if I would see her again. But when I looked up, she was gone.

I finally heard her say, "I'll be around. Like you, I ain't got no place else to go.

Chapter 14

MAMA AND FRANK slept the rest of the day and into the night. When mama got up to get a glass of water she said, "Frank, come in here a minute."

"What is it?" He groaned.

"Can you believe that little shit never come in and eat his sandwich?" said Mama.

"You sure?"

I'M TIMMY

"Well, here it sets, right chere on the table. Man, I'm gonna tan his hide when he gets in here."

She stomped to the door and opened it yelling, "Timothy Allen you get your ass in this house right now! Timothy? You hear me?"

She opened the door to my room. "Frank? When have you ever known Timothy to make his bed?"

"Never, that little bastard wouldn't piss on himself if he was on fire, much less make his own bed."

Then how come his beds made? It looks like he ain't slept in it atall. Go see if he's outside."

Frank mumbled, "I'm gonna beat the head off that boy when I find him. It's too damn cold to be traipsin' around after him."

"Go next door and see if he's over there." Mama ordered.

Frank made his way over to the neighbor's house. He knocked on the door.

"Miss Wilson," he said real nice, "I'm sorry to bother you, but have you seen my boy, Timmy?"

"Why, no, I haven't. Ain't seen hide nor hair of him and I been home all day." Said Miss Wilson.

Mama didn't like Miss Wilson; she said she was too nosy. So, if anybody'd seen me, it'd been Miss Wilson.

T. S. Kincaid

I followed Frank around half the night listening to him yell for me. I would've said something, but I thought it was funny watching him keep falling in all that piled up snow and freezing his ass off.

When he finally made it back to the house, mama was on the phone.

"Listen here, bitch. I said I need this line now get off of it. This is an emergency."

The woman musta paid no mind to mama 'cause she kept right on talkin'.

"Ida Stokes, get the hell off of this line. I can't find my boy and I need to call the police."

Ida Stokes said, "Since when are you so concerned for your boy? He's probally run off as mean as you are to him."

"You bitch! I'm gonna beat the hell outta you!" Screamed Mama. "Now get off the damn line."

Finally, Ida Stokes and whoever she was talkin' to hung up.

"Sherriff's office? This is Lou Ann Walker; I need you to get over to Frank's place right away. My boy Timothy's missin'"

Mama heard Ida Stokes whisper, "it's true, she really did call the police." Before she hung up.

I'M TIMMY

Frank looked pissed. "Now what the hell did you go and do that for?"

"Do what?" Mama said.

"Call my damn superiors. You shoulda give me some time to figure things out."

"Figure what out, Frank?"

"Yeah, Frank?" I wanted to know, too.

"I heard you the first time, woman." Maybe he's starting to hear me, but doesn't realize it's me.

"Timothy did come home last night, didn't he?" Mama asked

"Course he did. I said he did, didn't I?"

You did? Now I was getting' pissed. Why would he lie like that? You never even thought about coming to look for me. You didn't even know I was gone. The angrier I got, the colder Mama and Frank got. Mama started shivering and pulled her house coat up close around her neck. I saw Frank's teeth start to chatter.

"I just meant the little shit is probally off hidin' somewheres. I just needed some time to try and find him."

"What did you do?" Mama asked.

"Nothin'!" Frank yelled.

Mama started to say something else when not one but two police patrol cars rolled up in the driveway.

"Go get some damn clothes on," Frank whispered to Mama. He grabbed her by her arm, but she jerked away.

"Mike, Steve, Ya'll come on in," said Mama.

Mama went over everything she knew. It was amazing. It was as if I could see inside her mind and I could read all of her thoughts.

She was at the diner yesterday and saw that the storm was coming. Frank was supposed to come and pick her up after I got off the bus, but the weather was turning too bad. So, she called Frank and told him that the roads were getting too slick and that she was going to stay the night at the diner, so she could be there to open up this morning.

She asked Frank if I was home and he said "Yes." Then the phone went dead. She said she tried to call back a time or two but figured the storm had knocked the lines down. She stayed the night there and when they didn't have any business, they closed the diner and Al, her boss, brought her home.

"Does Al have a last name? The officer, I think his name is Mike, asked.

"Bixby," Mama said.

"And Al can verify all of this?" Mike asked.

Mama shook her head yes.

I'M TIMMY

"So, why did it take you so long to call us?" This must be Steve.

"Cause when I got here, nobody was home and I figured they was together. But Frank said Timothy had left long before he come to get me and I thought he was out playin.'"

"I thought you said, Al brought you home."

"He did. Frank said that's where he was when I asked him where he'd been."

"Okay, so what's your story, Frank?"

"What do you mean?" Frank was stalling. He knew he had to think of something to explain why he didn't know I hadn't come home.

"Okay guys, I admit I did a little drinkin' last night and I may have been out of it when he come home."

"Are you shitin' me?" Mama yelled. "You swore you's gonna lay off that stuff."

"So, what did you do with him?" Steve asked.

"Nothin'"

"Then where is he?"

"I don't know."

"Okay," said Mike. "Let's take a little ride down to the station."

Frank breathed a big sigh and gave Mama a mean glance.

Mama's eyes filled with tears and she said she would go and get dressed.

"No, that's okay. Just Frank for now. If we have any more questions, we'll let you know."

Frank left with the officers, and I stayed with Mama. She crawled back into her bed and started crying.

"It's okay, Mama. I'm here. I'm fine, really. Now we can always be together. I know how you hate to be alone."

I reached over to stroke mama's hair, but she jumped and scooted over to the far side of the bed.

"What the hell is that?" Mama's eyes scanned the room. "Get away from me!! Get away!" Mama was screaming so loud that I was sure the neighbors could hear her.

The dogs across the river started barking, then farther on down the way. It was as if they were spreading the news of the house where the crazy woman lived whose kid had disappeared.

I backed off and waited until Mama fell asleep.

"Klara? Klara, are you there?" I thought as hard as I could.

Finally, I could hear Klara's voice inside of my head.

I'M TIMMY

"What do you want?"

"No matter how hard I try, my Mama still can't hear me."

"Sometimes, they don't want to hear us."

"Not my Mama, she wouldn't do that." I insisted.

"Then your just gonna have to get good and mad."

I couldn't hear Klara anymore after that. I guess she has other things to do.

Since Frank hadn't come back yet, I decided to see what was going on with him.

Frank was sitting in a small room with a single light directly above his table. The two police officers were sitting on the opposite side of him.

"Okay, Frank, let's take it from the top."

"Jesus Crist, you guys are breakin' my balls here."

"Just tell us what happened." Mike said.

"I told you already, nothin."

"Look, you sneaky bastard, I know you did something. Now spill it." Steve slammed his hand down on the table and ran his fingers through his thick black hair.

Mike looked over at Steve and said, "Hey, it's been a long night. Let's just everybody take a break and settle down. Steve lets you and me go get a cup of coffee. Frank, we'll be right back."

"Sure thing."

Steve and Mike walked out of the room. I sat down in front of Frank. He shivered, and picked up a cigarette from the pack sitting on the table and placed it between his teeth. He struck the match. I blew it out. He struck another one. I blew it out again.

"Damn drafty place." He cupped his hands around the flame. This time I allowed him to light it.

His mind started drifting back to the day before. Instantly, I was transported by his thoughts as if watching a picture show from an old projector.

We sat in Mama's car at the end of Maple Street. Frank slowly drove by house number One Twenty-three. The patrol car was still parked in the driveway. 'Son of a bitch must be runnin' late today'. I could hear every thought as if he were talking out loud.

He drove to the dead end and turned around. He waited under a leafless maple tree. The car idling. He lit one cigarette after the other, becoming more frustrated as he finished each one flicking the butts onto the sidewalk. He sat up when he saw the brim of the black hat duck inside the patrol car. A lady came from the house and around to the passenger's side. It was the same woman I'd seen before. The one who'd been at our house and the one who'd been talking to Frank at the gas station.

When the patrol car pulled out, Frank waited until he saw the back taillights turn the corner before putting the car in drive. He pulled up to the front of the house and honked the horn. The pretty teenager I saw in the car with her mother pulled the curtain back and waved.

Seconds later she came barreling down the front steps and ran up and got in the car.

"Hi ya lover," she said as she scooted as far as she could next to Frank. She kissed him on the cheek reached up and nibbled on his ear.

Frank drove down to the river's edge. He put the car in park.

The girl straddled Frank and began sliding her tongue in and out of his mouth.

"Frankie," she said as she looked in his eyes. "Can't we go somewheres else this time?"

"Why baby? I thought you liked it here."

"I do," she said between kisses, "It's just that it is so cold this time of year. Can't we get a room or go someplace nice for once."

"I told you already Judy, since your daddy put me on suspension, I can't afford to take you anywhere. If your little bratty friend hadn't run her damn mouth, I wouldn't be in this trouble and be under investigation, now, would I?"

"How was I to know she was going to say you assaulted her? You know Frank, rumor has it that she was not the only one."

"Are you tryin' to piss me off?"

"No, no baby. I'm sorry. Let's just forget I ever said anything."

She began kissing him again. She was going from side to side on his face and sticking her tongue in his ear. He put his hand underneath her blouse and he started fondling her breast. She unbuttoned his shirt and kissed him on his chest, then his stomach, then she slipped her hand down in his pants and started rubbing him between the legs.

Frank reached down and unzipped his pants. Judy put her head between his legs and he started moaning. He was bouncing the seat up and down, when he said, "Oh, baby, let's get in the back."

Frank climbed over the seat and Judy followed. They both stretched out across the back seat, continuing to kiss and rub their hands up and down each other. Frank slipped his hand down between Judy's legs.

I'M TIMMY

"Damn baby, your so wet!" He smiled. "Good God, the wettest I have ever felt. I can't wait to get inside of you."

Judy smiled as she slipped off her underpants. Frank removed his hand and placed it up around her head. He suddenly jumped up.

"Shit!" He yelled. "Why didn't you tell me you were on the rag?"

"Oh, come on baby, it don't matter." Said Judy grabbing his shirt and trying to pull him back down to her.

"The hell it don't." Frank said. "That shit turns me right off." He took his blood-soaked hand and tried to wipe it off underneath and on the back of the seat. He clamored back over the seat and told Judy to put her damn clothes back on. They rode in silence all the way back to Judy's house. Frank pulled up to her front door and sped away without as much as a goodbye when she got out. The door shut itself as he sped away.

Frank went back to his house and started frantically looking for something. The snow began falling outside. He checked every cupboard and shelf. At last, just when he was about to give up, he spotted it. The black tip of the bottle of bourbon stuck out right behind the sack of flour.

"Ha, you bitch, I knew you still had some."

He opened the bottle and drank it straight. His eyes were red and watery, and soon, he was staggering around. He lay down on the couch and was just drifting off when the phone rang. Frank managed to get it before the last ring. It was Mama telling him that because of the storm, she was going to be staying over at the diner. I heard her ask about me, and he said, yeah, just before the phone went dead.

Frank staggered back over to the couch and passed out. The only time he budged was when there was an explosion and he raised his head and said, "What the hell was that?"

Mike and Steve reentered the room. Frank was sitting there shivering.

"Damn, don't you guys ever pay the power bill in this place? It's freezing."

I stood directly beside Frank, not giving him a break from the cold. Mike picked up Frank's pack of cigarettes. He handed one to Frank, gave him a light, then lit his own.

"Come on Frankie, you and me go way back. Just tell us what you did with the kid."

I'm Timmy

"I swear to God, Mike. I didn't do nothing to the kid."

"That's right," I screamed. "You did nothing! I waited and waited for you! You should have come for me! I had a life. I had the right to live. It you hadn't been out screwing around and getting drunk we wouldn't be here right now. This is your fault Frank Walker and for that you're gonna pay."

"Who the hell is that?" Frank said.

Aw, so he could hear me. This is gonna be fun.

Mike and Steve just looked at each other.

"I'm gonna get you, Frank." I yelled.

"Hey guys, cut it out! You can't scare me."

Mike whispered in Steve's ear. "Maybe he's trying to play the looney card. Just play along. Maybe he'll slip up."

"Sorry, Frank. We don't hear nothin'. Maybe it's your conscience talking to ya."

Frank listened again, but I stayed silent.

He leaned back in his chair and laced his fingers between his hands. "Maybe the little idiot fell in a hole somewheres between the bus stop and home."

As soon as he finished his sentence, I pulled his chair legs, and he fell to the ground, smacking his head on the cement floor. He got up and looked around, confused.

"Look guys, I'm one of you," he finally said.

"You're not one of us, you piece of shit." Steve interrupted.

"Whatever. I know the drill. You ain't got nothin' so you gotta let me go."

Mike and Steve looked at each other. Steve took a deep breath and said, "You're right, for now."

Chapter 15

AS SOON AS Frank came home, he saw mama sitting on the couch.

"Where's the damn car?" Frank asked.

"They came this morning and took it," Mama said coldly.

"Took it where?"

"To impound, you asshole." She stated.

"Why the hell would they take it to impound?"

T. S. Kincaid

Mama didn't have an answer. The phone rang.

"Good God, you get it this time. The damn thing has been ringin' off the hook all day."

"Well, who the hells been callin?"

"Who hasn't? People wantin' to know what happened. People wantin' to know if we found him yet. People wantin' to know if they can join the search party. People wantin' to know if I need posters. The newspaper wantin' the latest picture of him, askin' what he was wearin'. The Chronicle- Journal from Louisville wants to come out here to do an interview. Blah, blah, blah. I am so sick to death of hearin' about it."

Mama, it's only been a day or two. Don't you care about what's happened to me? Don't you wonder where I am?

"Course I care where he's at. Why in the world would you ask such a thing?"

Hey! Maybe I am getting through to her.

Frank looked at her confused. "Who the hell you talkin' to?"

"Just forget it." Said Mama.

Maybe not, I thought.

That evening the police returned to the house. Frank was sittin' at the table smokin', when they knocked on the door.

"What now?" Frank said.

"We're gonna need you to come back down to the police station, we have some more questions we want to ask you."

"Look guys, I've already answered all of your questions, now you're startin' to harass me."

"Get your ass up and get in the car. I'm not playing with you!" Steve said.

When the neighbor saw the police cars, they all gathered outside. A reporter from the newspaper was also there.

"Mr. Walker, where is your stepson?" The reporter asked.

"What did you do to himm?" Someone shouted from the crowd.

"Is he still alive?' A woman yelled.

"Child killer!" Another screamed.

For once Frank kept his mouth shut and ducked into the patrol car.

I couldn't stand it and had to know what Frank would say, so I joined them.

At the station, Mike and Steve were not as friendly as they were the first time.

"Okay, dickhead, you need to fess up. Where's the kid?"

"I already told you; I don't know!"

"We got a witness saying that your car was spotted down by the river on the day he disappeared. What were you doing down there?' Steve asked.

Frank started to say, "Screwing your daughter." But he didn't.

"And where did you go on the day his mother reported him missing? No one saw you go over to the diner."

"Look we got a teacher, a principal, and a kid all saying he got on the bus that day. Now where the hell is he?"

"Look, I already told you. I don't know how else to put it to make you morons understand. I don't know where the kid is. I did not see him. I did not take him. Or do anythin' to hurt him. Now, I'm goin' home.

"Fraid not", Mike said, "We found blood on the back seat and floorboard of your car"

Frank looked puzzled. Then he remembered. Judy. "Look, I can explain that. But not right now."

"Put your hands behind your back. Frank Walker, you are under arrest for the murder of Timothy Thomson."

I was as shocked as Frank when they put the handcuffs on him. He kept screamin' and yellin' to anyone who would listen, "I didn't do it, I'm tellin' you!"

But no one listened, and if they did, they didn't care. Frank was hauled off to the Franklin County jail.

Mama was on the phone again, this time talking to Uncle Bob.

"No, we still ain't heard nothin'. It's been almost three days now. Where could he be? People have been looking all over for him. Mama paused and listened to Uncle Bob.

"Yes, he's at the police station now. They took him down there for more questioning. Well, of course I'm scared. What if he comes back here? I just know he did somethin' to Timothy." More silence.

"Bob, he told me Timothy came home that night. I asked him straight out. What am I gonna do if they let him go?"

A car door slammed.

"Oh, God! He's back, I better go."

Mama put the phone down and went to the window. It was Mike from the police station.

"I wanted to come here and tell you personally. We arrested Frank for the murder of Timothy."

Mama swooned. Mike caught her and helped her to the couch.

"Do you really think he did it?" She asked Mike after he got her a glass of water.

"Looks that way. We have called off the search."

A slight smile crept across Mama's face.

I could tell she was happy, and rightly so. Now she would not have to worry about Frank. At least for a while.

Turns out she decided to do the interview with the news after all. She spent hours in her room getting ready. She sat at her make-up table putting her face on. Then she did something strange. She started talking to herself in the mirror.

"I'd like to thank the academy for choosing my life story as best picture. Of course, everyone knows the tale of my son Timothy's tragic murder, and that I barely escaped with my own life from that brut of an ex-husband of mine.

No, wait, let me try that again.

I know my loving husband is innocent. He'd never do nothin'' to hurt my beloved son, Timothy. Timothy, I know you're still out there. We're waiting for you, honey. Mama loves you. I even decided to keep the tree up and not to open any presents until his safe return…she looked at herself and smiled. "Yeah, that's good."

Now, what is she doing? Practicing crying? Oh Mama, you sure do act strange sometimes. What tree? What presents?

I was amazed to see all of the people who cared about finding out what happened to me. People came from miles around, taking time away from their own families. Going out into the bitter cold just to see if they could find me. There were newspaper articles and bits of news on TV.

Of course, all kinds of rumors spread like a disease. One person said I'd been kidnapped and was being held in a fallout shelter. One said Frank had murdered me and thrown me into the river. Another said he had chopped me up into little pieces and buried me in the backyard.

It's funny how I could go my whole life invisible to most people, but when I die, or people think I'm dead, everyone suddenly knows my name.

I wondered where everyone was before all of this happened and why no one ever bothered to come to my rescue when I was alive. It made me angry and resentful.

T. S. Kincaid

The town was split on two sides about Frank. The ones who thought he was innocent held up signs outside the jail demanding he be set free, while others wanted to have an old-fashioned lynching and get justice right then and there.

Seemed like the whole town was nice to mama. She ate it up. She'd cry, or act really sad whenever she thought people was around, but I noticed her mood changed when she was alone. She didn't act like she missed me. Maybe that was just Mama's way.

I had heard many of the rumors, thanks to the party line, but I decided to go and pay Susan a visit. Had she given any thought to what was going on?

Susan was in her bedroom playing with her paper dolls, acting like she didn't have a care in the world. Hadn't she heard about the accident at the school? Her mother knocked, then opened the bedroom door.

"Susan, dear, you have a visitor."

Susan looked up surprised, then smiled. It was Mrs. Calhoun.

Ah good. Now, the truth will come out. I just stood there in the corner of her room, invisible.

I'm Timmy

"Hi, Susan. Since we're neighbors, Mr. Richards asked me if I would mind dropping off some of your assignments until school resumes. I told him I'd be glad to." Smiled Mrs. Calhoun.

"Have you heard any word about how they are going to handle all of this mess?" Susan's mother asked.

"Not yet." Answered Mrs. Calhoun.

"Isn't that just awful about the Thomson boy?" Asked Susan's mother.

"Oh yes, I nearly cried my eyes out when I heard the news. Such a sweet little boy, and so popular. I hope they hang that Step-daddy of his out to dry." Mrs. Calhoun lied.

Shame on you Mrs. Calhoun. If I was such a sweet little boy, why did you treat me the way you did? I could feel the anger starting to stir inside of me.

"Ooo, it feels a bit nippy in here." Said Susan's mother. "I'll have to turn up the heat."

"I did have a few things I wanted to speak with Susan about, about her assignments, that is."

"Oh, of course. I'll leave you two alone. Congratulations." Susan's mother winked at Mrs. Calhoun and then left, closing the door behind her.

Mrs. Calhoun rushed over to Susan and quietly sat beside her on the bed.

"Listen, now this is very important. Did you see Timothy Thomson get on that bus?" She whispered.

"Timothy Thomson? Oh, you mean the boy who's missing? Now let me see."

Susan tilted her head and looked up toward the ceiling, like she was thinking really hard, trying to remember.

"Uh, I think so." She finally said.

Mrs. Calhoun grabbed her by the arms and squeezed them tight. "Think! Now this is very important, you've got to be sure."

Tears welled up in Susan's frightened eyes. "You're hurting me."

Mrs. Calhoun loosened her grip. "I'm sorry, but I really need to know. Now, please try to think."

"We were all standin' there together." Susan sniffed. "I mean, he must have gotten on, right? At least, that's what I told the police."

"The police questioned you?"

"Why sure, I mean, I think they questioned everybody, right?"

"You didn't say anything about me leaving early, did you?"

"Oh! No Ma'am!" Susan crossed her heart with her fingers. "I promised you I wouldn't and I didn't."

Mrs. Calhoun let out a huge sigh of relief.

"Okay, that's fine. Nothing to worry about." Mrs. Calhoun seemed to say that more to herself, than to Susan. "I would appreciate it if you wouldn't say a word about anything we have talked about here today."

"Okay." Susan looked confused. "I'm not in any sort of trouble, am I?"

"No, of course not. Everything is fine. Just remember, not a word to anyone." Mrs. Calhoun stood and put her finger to her lips.

Susan looked at Mrs. Calhoun and crossed her heart again.

"I have to go now. See you later."

I followed Mrs. Calhoun into the living room, where she stopped to speak with Susan's mother again.

She was offered a cup of tea, but said she needed to be getting home.

I decided to revisit that day. The day of my death, before the fire. I saw myself standing on that snow-covered sidewalk, waiting to see if Mrs. Calhoun was going to let me go back into the building. She was talking to Susan about making sure everyone got on the bus. Mrs. Calhoun waved me away and told me to "make it quick." Susan had turned away before that and was talking to her friend Peggy. Of course. Susan did not see Mrs. Calhoun tell me to go back into the building. So, she didn't know. Susan didn't know. She was not to blame.

But you knew, didn't you, Mrs. Calhoun? You knew you let me go back into that building and left before you found out if I came back out.

So, what are you doing here? You're trying to cover your ass, aren't you? What did you do? Figure out the real story about what happened and now you're afraid you'll get the blame for it? Are you to blame? Maybe.

The more I thought about it, the angrier I got. I thought of all of the mean things that Mrs. Calhoun had done to me. The many times she made me feel like a fool.

I waited outside for Mrs. Calhoun. She finally came out and walked across the lawn to her own home.

The inside of her house was bright and cheerful. She took off her coat and went into the kitchen to put a teapot of water on the stove.

She replayed the scene of that day again in her mind. Then I saw her at the doctor's office. I saw when she got the news. She smiled. I could hear her thinking to herself, it was worth leaving early that day. Now I have wonderful news to tell Carl. I guess that was her husband.

Wonderful news? Awe yes, the baby. I could hear the whoosh, whoosh, whoosh of his rapid heartbeat. I stood across from Mrs. Calhoun while she waited for her pot to boil. She shivered and rubbed her hands up and down her arms just like she did that cold day on the sidewalk.

I reached over and turned off the stove's gas. She went back to the stove and clicked the pilot over and over. The flame wouldn't restart. She bent her face down near the stove when suddenly the flame leaped into the air. I put my face through the flame and said, "Hi, Mrs. Calhoun."

She gasped and backed away so quickly, she fell against the kitchen sink. She tried to escape through the kitchen door, but I blocked her.

She ran upstairs screaming the whole way. When she got in her bedroom, she slammed the door and locked it. She was leaning against the door, panting.

I knocked. "Mrs. Cal-hou-n," I said. It's your sweet little Timothy, may I come in?"

"No, no!" She screamed. "Go away and leave me alone!"

"Oh, please? I just want to talk to you." I softly said.

She continued screaming.   She ran over to her dresser and struggled to push it against the door.

 I stood beside her and said, "Here, let me help."

I pushed the heavy dresser across the room. It slid across that wooden floor like warm butter on toast, slamming up against the door. I was amazed by my own strength.

"Mrs. Calhoun, I think it's time you go to your corner," I said while I pushed on her back. Her feet slid to the other side of the room. I put my hand on the back of her neck and made sure she could not turn around.

"Now you stay there until I say you can sit back down, understand?"

She stood there quivering in the corner.

I pulled on her ear.

"Is there any wax in there?" I asked. "Because you're not answering me." I released my grip.

She started shaking uncontrollably. "You get away from me, you!" she turned and swatted at the air. "What do you want?"

I'M TIMMY

I thought about it for a minute. What *did* I want? I wanted a lot of things. I wanted to be able to talk to my mama and for her to be able to hear me. I wanted Frank to go away forever. But most of all, I wanted my life back. I wanted to live again. To grow up, to be who I was supposed to be, and not some damn ghost who has nothing and no one who loves him to talk to.

"I want to live again!" I screamed.

"But, but what can I do about that?" She yelled. "I can't do anything about that now."

"If I can't have my life back, then I'll take one." I flew all through the room, banging on her windows and doors. Turning her lights on and off.

She fell to her knees begging me, "Oh, please, please, don't kill me! I'm going to have a baby. Please don't hurt me. I'm sorry! I'm so, so sorry! Think of how your own mother feels. Killing me won't bring you back."

"You're right," I said, "Yours was not the life I was planning on taking."

"Oh, no, no!" She screamed.

She somehow managed to move that dresser and unlock the door. Before I knew it, she was running down the hallway.

T. S. Kincaid

She tripped on the rug at the top of her stairs and tumbled down them.

I stood at the top of the stairs looking down at her twisted legs. She began to moan and move her head.

Rage fueled my body, which exposed a flame as I came down the stairs. My skin was melting like a candle dripping wax. That beam that crushed my head made my eye pop out. It was hanging by the threads of tendons and veins. The flames lit up my charred and blistered body.

I bent down over Mrs. Calhoun and in my half mumbling/half whispering voice I said, "Mrs. Calhoun, you are a nasty, awful, person. You don't deserve to be a mother. You don't deserve to be a teacher."

"You were my *teacher*," my voice got louder. "Someone who was supposed to make sure I was nurtured and grew. Someone who was supposed to protect me and help me when my parents weren't around. Someone who believed in me and made me feel like I could do anything I set my mind to."

"But instead," I screamed, "you were nothing but a big bully who cut me down every chance you got. And for what? Just because you didn't like me for something I never did? You didn't have to like me, Mrs. Calhoun, but you didn't have to treat me the way you did either!

I'M TIMMY

Why are you so willing to let Frank take the blame for something that was your fault? Give me one good reason why I should let you live."

"Ahhh," she screamed. "Please, please…" Her eyes were wild. She was desperately searching the room, refusing to look at me.

She finally said, "You're right! I'm sorry! I'm so, so, sorry. Oh! Please, please. I know it was my fault. I know I never should have given Susan that responsibility. I promise you; I promise I will be better from now on. Please, just give me one more chance. Don't you see? I was so excited. Carl! My husband Carl, all he wants is a baby. That's all he talks about. Please, he's such a good man. If not for me, do it for him."

At that moment, I thought of my own daddy. He was a good man. Maybe Carl was a lot like him. Maybe Carl could give this baby a good life like my father tried to give me.

"What about you? Do you want this baby?" I glared.

"Yes!"

"I can read your mind, you know."

"Yes, I swear! Please…"

T. S. Kincaid

I looked deep into her eyes. She was telling the truth.

She lay there weeping.

I couldn't hear the whoosh, whoosh, whoosh.

"No!" I shouted.

She covered her stomach with her hands. I guess she was afraid I was gonna hurt her.

I was only trying to scare her. It was an accident. I wasn't really going to hurt her or her baby. I felt so bad. I stood there for the longest time, wondering what to do. I couldn't call anyone. No one would even know it was me who was to blame. Even if she told someone, who was going to believe her?

I thought of the pain I caused her. Not just the pain in her body, but the pain she and her husband would feel in their heart. The pain of knowing they would never have the baby they wanted. And it was all my fault. I would be the blame. Even if no one ever knew it was me, I knew. I was so ashamed that I turned invisible again.

I moved closer to her.

Wait.

What was that?

I heard it. It was faint, but it was there.

Whoosh, whoosh, whoosh.

I'M TIMMY

I had to get help, but how?

I looked all around. Then I remembered she had an old-timey bell outside of her house. You know, like the ones they used to have to ring when school was being open or let out? It also subbed for a church bell. I guess with her being a teacher and all she thought it made a great decoration.

I grabbed that bell and started ringing it as loud and as fast as it would ring. I rang that bell until all of the neighbors ran from their houses to see what was going on.

They all came running. They ran up on her porch beating and banging on the door. I opened it.

When a man saw her lying on the floor, he called for help.

Soon, an ambulance came and loaded her into the back. The whoosh, whoosh, whoosh was stronger now.

"Mrs. Calhoun," I said in her car. "I hope you APPRECIATE that I let you and your baby live. I'll be watching you, so don't you forget your promise."

She had an oxygen mask over her face, so she crossed her heart instead.

Everything would be okay.

At least for them.

Chapter 16

MAMA WAS ON the phone yet again when I returned home. I wanted to tell her about all of the excitement and I wondered if she would be proud of me. Not for harmin' Mrs. Calhoun or almost killin' her baby, but for standin' up for myself and no longer bein' a scaredy cat. She just might be impressed with all of the things I can do now, but I'm still a scaredy cat when it comes to her. I wouldn't want to do anything to make her not love me.

I'm Timmy

I overheard her talkin' to Uncle Bob. He said he and the family would be making the trip up here to Kentucky to give Mama moral support. Mama told him she refused to go to the jail to see Frank and did not plan to attend his trial. She thought maybe it wouldn't look good, her bein' there. At the trial, I mean.

"Well, Lou Ann, I think that's best." Said Uncle Bob.

"But what if he gets off?" Asked Mama. "Then what will I do if he wants to come back here."

Then I would take care of him, I told Mama.

"Oh, Bob, be serious. How are you gonna take care of him? He's way bigger and meaner than you are."

"Sorry," said Uncle Bob, "You lost me. Anyways we'll see you in a couple of days."

I was still not getting' through to Mama. She could hear my words, but for some reason she was still not understandin' it was me who was talkin' and not someone else. Maybe tonight when she's sleepin' I can try again. In the meantime, I may just pop in on Aunt Erma and see what she was up to.

I found her in the beauty parlor.

"Oh yes, the whole thing is such a tragedy. My poor, poor nephew. Murdered by his step-father and he won't tell anyone where the body is."

"Well, if there is no body, then how do they know he murdered him?" The lady combing Aunt Erma's hair asked.

"Of course he murdered him. They found blood covering the whole back seat of his car. If that doesn't say he done it, then I don't know what does. Oh! That Timmy was the sweetest little thing. I just loved him to death. My boy, Larry is just so heartbroken over this whole mess, I think I am going to let him stay with my sister in Brookhaven. She is going to take him to the big Christmas parade over there."

Great! Larry gets to go to a Christmas parade, and I get to be dead.

As I sat there listening to all of her lies, I began to think of all of the mean things she'd said about Daddy. When the hair dresser went into the back room to mix up Aunt Erma's hair dye, I followed her. I looked around at all of the products and there, on the top shelf in the back I found somethin' that I thought would be perfect.

When the lady mixin' the dye went to answer the telephone, I poured about half a bottle of hair remover into the mix.

I returned to sit in the chair next to Erma.

I'M TIMMY

The hairdresser came out from the back room and started puttin' that mixture on Aunt Erma's head.

"Hey, watch it. This stuff is startin' to burn." Aunt Erma complained.

"Oh, don't be such a ninny. That's perfectly normal. Now just sit still, this will only take a little while." Said the lady as she continued to pour the mixture all over Aunt Erma's head.

"Okay, now come on over here to this dryer and we can let that set for a while."

"Hey, I'm not kiddin' this stuff is really burnin'" Erma's eyes started waterin',

The lady just kept working on the other customer and acted like she couldn't hear Erma, no matter how much she complained.

Erma sat there under that big hair dryer sweatin' and frettin' to beat the band.

Finally, I guess she couldn't take it no more, 'cause she started screamin' at that lady and makin' an awful scene.

'Get it off me! Get it off me!" She screamed over and over.

The woman rushed over and tried to lift the dryer off of Erma's burnin' head, but couldn't.

I don't think my sittin' on top of it helped. Finally, I decided she had had enough and climbed down from the top of the dryer.

The woman lifted the lid and rushed Erma over to the sink as fast as she could.

As she was warshin' her hair, her eyes got huge, and she looked like she was scared to death.

Massive amounts of Erma's hair was fallin' out and swirling down the drain, hair dye and all.

"What's wrong?"

Erma must have seen the woman's face. The woman quickly grabbed a towel and threw it over Erma's head.

"There must have been some kind of mistake," the woman started.

Erma quickly yanked the towel from her head. She ran to a mirror and began screamin'. Then she fainted. All of the people in the shop ran over to try to get her to wake up. Some woman pulled a bottle from her pocketbook and said to place it under her nose. They kept it under her nose until she finally opened her eyes.

Erma placed her hands on her partly bald head and ran to the mirror again.

The lady who was doin' her hair kept sayin', "I'm so sorry, I don't know what happened."

I'M TIMMY

The hairdresser went back to the back room and saw the bottle of hair remover on the counter. She quickly threw it in the trash. When she returned to the front of the shop, Erma was still standin' in front of the mirror screamin'.

Erma lunged at the woman and started chokin' her. The woman put her hands up to her throat trying to get Erma to release her grip. Other women in the shop jumped up to help the woman.

Erma started screamin', "I'm gonna kill you! I will wipe this floor with you," and other stupid stuff like that.

All of the people in the shop got together and forced Erma out the door. She stood out on the street and kept right on screamin' and jumping up and down. She was grabbing the arms of strangers and sayin' look what that woman did to me!

She finally got in her car and sped away before the cops arrived.

I'll tell you, that was really somethin' to see. I laughed so hard I surely would have peed my pants if I could.

I rode with Erma to the local drug store. She ran up to the man behind the counter and asked what she could put on her blistered head. The man sort of snickered and then told her where the burn cream was while tryin' to keep a straight face.

Erma looked so funny. Most of her hair was gone. Just little pieces stickin' out here and there. The rest of her head was blistered and red. After she got the medicine, she went home and cried herself to sleep.

I returned home to Mama.

She was her usual cheerful self. Going around the house singin' with the radio while she did some cleanin'. I tried a few times to talk to her. She stopped, like maybe she heard me, but then she just shook her head and kept on doin' what she was doin'."

That night I waited until Mama was good and asleep. I crawled up in the bed and snuggled up real close.

"Mama?" I said. "Mama, I love you, and I am here with you all the time. Anytime you want to talk to me all you have to do is say something."

Mama just kept on takin' deep breaths in and out.

"I miss you." I said.

"I miss you, too, Frank." She finally said.

I'M TIMMY

Oh Mama, I wish I understood what was wrong with you. I went into the other room and waited on the couch for the rest of the night.

The next evening Uncle Bob arrived alone. He said Aunt Erma weren't feelin' well and decided not to come. He never did say nothin' 'bout Erma's hair or her blisters.

He and Mama spent the night drinkin' beers and talkin' 'bout when they was kids. I listened for a while, but got tired of hearin' bout how many boyfriends Mama had and how many fights Uncle Bob had to get into on her behalf.

I got to thinkin' bout Eddie and Beau. For the first time, I did not have any fear about seein' 'em. When I got to their room, I decided to hang out for a little while just to see what was goin' on.

Both of the brother's came into their room and began getting ready for bed. Eddie took off his t-shirt and climbed onto the top bunk. He got a magazine from under his pillow and turned on his flashlight as he opened it to the centerfold.

"Hey!" Said Beau, "I wanted to see too!"

T. S. Kincaid

"Keep your voice down, dumbass, do you want mom or pop to come in here?"

"Let me see!" demanded Beau as he tried to grab the magazine.

"No! Get your stinkin' paws off!" Eddie smacked Beau's hand away.

Beau kept grabbin' for the magazine and tore one of the pages.

Eddie rolled it up and swatted his brother on the head with it.

"Ow!" Beau yelled. " Give it to me!"

Eddie jumped on Beau's back and they both fell to the floor with a thump. They began wrestlin' around.

"If you boys know what's good for you, you will settle down in there and get to bed." Their father yelled from the livin' room.

They kept bangin' around and hittin' each other. Eddie got on top of Beau and pinned him down. Beau kicked Eddie between the legs which made him roll over and scream in pain. I hid under the bed and created a shadow. Beau stopped and stared right at me.

"Hey! There's somethin' under there." Beau told his brother.

"Shup-up, stupid." Snapped Eddie.

"No, I'm serious. There's somethin' under my bed."

I began to growl a low growl.

"What the hell?" said Beau, as he put his hand under the bed. I grabbed his hand and bit him real hard. He screamed in pain.

The door burst open and the light was switched on. Mr. Roger's came rushin' in the room with a belt in his hand.

He struck Beau first.

"Get up off the damn floor you idgit, and get your ass in that bed." He screamed.

He kept hittin' him on the butt with the thick leather strap.

Eddie quickly climbed back in his top bunk and tried to cover up the magazine.

"What are you tryin' to hide, you little bastard?"

"Nuthin!" Eddied lied.

Mr. Rogers grabbed at the pillow that Eddie had in front of him.

"So, that's what happened to my magazine!" He began smackin' Eddie with the belt. "This is not for you, you little perverts! Keep your grubby hands off of it, Understand?"

"Yes, sir!" Cried Eddie.

T. S. Kincaid

"Now get your asses back in the bed and I don't want to hear another peep out of you, you got that?"

"Yes, sir!" Both boys said.

Mr. Rogers stormed out the door, slammin', it behind him.

Both boys were cryin' as Beau climbed up to the top bunk with Eddie.

"I swear somethin' was under my bed. Look where it bit me."

Eddie looked at the huge bite on his brother's arm.

I darted across the room and stood in the corner.

"Did you see that? I'm tellin' you man, somethin's in here."

Eddie quietly grabbed the flashlight. He turned it on and the dim light lit up a small section of the room. Both boys squinted their eyes to see.

"There! In the corner!" Beau whispered.

Eddie shinned the light in that direction, but sighed when he realized it was just a coat hangin' on a hook.

"They ain't nothin' in here. Just admit it, you were just shitin' me. Now, get the hell off my bed."

"No. I swear. There is somethin' in here. Please let me stay up here with you."

Beau sat sittin' at the edge of Eddie's bed.

I'm Timmy

"Look you little woos, I told you to get out of my bed. There is nothin' in here."

Eddie took the flashlight and shinned it once more around the room.

I climb up on the bed and sat between them.

I appeared as my normal self and said, "Hi fellows, remember me?"

Both boys looked shocked. Beau jumped off the bed and ran for the door.

I got in front of him and put my finger up to my lips.

"Shhh," I said, "this is our little game and no one else is invited."

Eddie jumped down and grabbed his younger brother. They both huddled together in the bottom bunk.

Eddie finally said, "Wwwwhat do you want?"

"Just to give you a taste of the same shit you give everyone else. Aren't you havin' fun?" I showed my dead self and got close to their faces. I could hear their hearts poundin' and see the fear in their eyes.

"I just want you to know, you two are goin' to straighten up. No more bullyin' or pickin' on people or anything else. I'll be watchin' you. Where ever you go, and whatever you get in to, I'll be there. You two think about that."

Beau and Eddie stayed up the rest of the night talkin' 'bout what had just happened.

"Have you ever been more scared in your whole life?" Eddie asked Beau.

"Do you think he is still here? Maybe we should turn the light on." Beau said.

"Pop would kill us if we sleep with the light on." Warned Eddie.

"Well, I can't sleep with it off. What if he comes back?"

"Whoever said I was gone?" I whispered.

They both jumped. I laughed so long and hard. Just like they used to laugh at me.

That ought to do it, I thought to myself. Surely they will be good now that I have given 'em a warnin'. I decided to go home and check on mama. I would come back to see 'em in a couple of days. Just to make sure they was bein' good.

Uncle Bob returned home and Aunt Erma's head was still sore, but was healin'. The doctor told her she would never grow hair again in some of those spots.

She laid on the couch and just howled. Uncle Bob tried to make her feel better by lying and tellin' her she was just as beautiful with or without hair. Erma was not fallin' for it though and kept tellin' him to shut-up.

Then Aunt Erma came home one day with the goofiest looking wig on. It was big and poofy and Uncle Bob just acted like she was the prettiest thing he'd ever seen. She ate it up. I guess you have to do what it takes to make the ones you love happy.

Mama was still bein' her silly self. Talkin' sometimes to people who weren't there. I know cause I couldn't see 'em. It was all in her head. I noticed that mama liked to pretend a lot. Maybe she was so unhappy in the world she lived in that she felt she had to make stuff up. I felt kind of sorry for her. I tried many nights in her dreams to let her know how much she was loved and that I would never leave her. Lots of nights she acted like that was not enough and she seemed to always be lookin' for something she just couldn't find.

Oh, don't worry. I'm not gonna give up on my Mama. I just have to love her more. She'll come around.

One evenin' I was lying there next to Mama while she watched T.V. She had been on the news and kept callin' all of the people she knew to see if they had seen it. She talked about how her hair looked and kept askin' did she really sound like that. She didn't seem to be too concerned that the Prosecutor was tryin' for the death penalty for Frank even though they still hadn't found my body.

As I was sittin' there, I got the strangest feelin'. Something was not right. Someone was in trouble. Real trouble. I had to find out who it was. I kept seein' flashes of Eddie and Beau. I went to their house, but they weren't there. I concentrated and found myself in the park. It was dusk and the streetlights were just startin' to come on.

I heard someone cryin'. But I didn't get the sense that it was one of them.

I heard it again. This time more desperate.

"Please let me go, I promise I won't tell anyone. I just want to go home. Please!"

It was a little girl, maybe five or six years old. She was over in the woods with Eddie and Beau. They had her pinned to the ground. She was scared and she had the same confused look that Sheba had had that day.

Someone was yellin' for her. "Susie, it's time to come in now."

Beau ripped off her underpants and shoved them into her mouth. "Don't you dare say a word."

Eddie put his hands around her throat.

I'M TIMMY

More people were startin' to come lookin' for her now. "Have you seen Susie?"

"Susie!" I could hear the panic in their voices.

Eddie started to squeeze her throat harder. She couldn't breath and I could feel she was startin' to pass out.

I quickly grabbed Eddie by his shirt and threw him over onto the grass. I picked up Beau and slung him over into the trees.

I picked up the little girl, Susie, and said "Run!"

Susie took off screamin' and cryin'. Her mother ran to her and picked her up in her arms. The crowd of people surrounded them as she carried her back home.

Beau was out cold. Eddie began to run when I caught him and took him over to the swings. I grabbed him by his shirt collar and pulled him up onto the swing. I stood behind him. I pulled the chains backward and forward, causin' the swing to pump higher and higher.

Back and forth, back and forth.

Eddie tried to escape, but I held his hands tightly against the chains and stood on his feet with them firmly on the wooden swing.

Back and forth, back and forth. Higher and higher we swung.

"What the hell man? Let me go!" Eddie shrieked.

T. S. Kincaid

We got higher and higher. We were swinging even with the bar the swings were attached to. Another street light came on.

I continued to pump harder and faster.

"Come on man! I said let me go!" Eddie insisted.

Now the swing was higher than the bar. The slack and tension of the chain kept moving back and forth.

"Come on, we're too high. It's gonna go over. Let me down!" Eddie screamed.

"You want me to let you go?" I asked.

"Yes, yes!"

"Are you sure?" I said.

"Yes! You bastard! Let me go!"

With that, I released my grip and Eddie fell as the chain wrapped around his neck. It snapped it like a string bean. His body dangled there swinging back and forth until it finally stopped.

The third street light came on.

I could see Eddie's shadow with his head tilted to one side.

I heard a scream and looked over towards the woods. Beau darted out and grabbed his bicycle.

I grabbed his handle bars. "Where do you think you're going?" I asked.

"We thought you were a dream!" Beau screamed.

I'm Timmy

"Oh, I'm a dream all right. Your worst nightmare."

Beau jumped on his bike and began to pedal faster and faster.

I sat in the middle of his handlebars. Jerking them quickly to the left then right.

"Watch it now, watch it." I teased. "Your gonna wreck."

"Leave me alone!" He screamed.

I kept jerking his handle bars and laughing in his face.

Faster and faster he raced. His legs barely being able to keep up.

"Get off of my bike!" He screamed.

"Okay," I said.

Boom!

Beau ran right into the side of that train, leaving nothing but a huge splattered mess.

"Wow!" I smiled. "I didn't even see that comin'."

Chapter 17

MAMA HAD NO choice but to go back to work at the diner. She still didn't have a car. The police said they were keepin' it for evidence. Not that it mattered cause she never did get her license anyways. All of the money that people had given her to help her out for the past few weeks had finally run out.

Soon enough Mama slipped back into her old ways. She was going out and stayin' out late at night with one man or the other. The difference was, now I could go with her when she went out instead of bein' stuck at home by myself.

At first, I was excited to go out with her. This way I could keep an eye out and keep her safe. After a while though, I realized mama could pretty much take care of herself. I didn't like goin' into bars and watchin' her rub up against all of these strange men. It made my stomach turn to watch her dancin' around showin' off her body and getting' stinkin' drunk. I wondered what Daddy would say.

Mama was lookin' old. Don't get me wrong, she was still beautiful, but I could see the small wrinkles startin' to show around her eyes and over the tops of her lips. She pretended like she was happy with all of these different men she went out with. But when we got home she would lay in the bed and cry. I tried to comfort her, but she would always seem to push me away.

After a while, I got tired of goin' out with Mama. I did like I did before. I stayed home and waited for her. Every now and then she would bring some stranger home. He'd rub all up against her and she'd smile like she was havin' the best time. But this was our time together, mine and mama's so I'd get sick of the man and have to scare him off.

One time I scared this man so bad he had a heart attack. Mama had to have another fight with Ida Stokes to get her to get off of the phone sos she could call for an ambulance. Turns out the man lived. Serves him right, he shouldn't have been messin' round with mama anyways.

Every now and then, I would go to the park to talk with Klara. She got me good one time. I went to the park and didn't see her. I called for her, but she didn't answer. A big gust of wind blew by and the swing started to move.

When I went to grab the swing, Klara said, "Now just what do you think you're a doin'? You know that this here is my swing."

"You got me," I smiled.

"Hey! I've been watchin' you. You're getting' a lot better. Things will get easier the longer you're here. Why I bet, in a hundred years or so, you will be almost as good as me."

A hundred years. Daddy was right. Eternity is a long time.

"I'm sorry," said Klara. I didn't mean to make you sad."

I'M TIMMY

"Oh, it's alright. Hey, Klara. I've been thinkin' 'bout Eddie and Beau."

"Oh, them. Why waste your time?" She asked.

"Well, It's just that I haven't seen 'em. I know if they was lookin' for me they'd be able to find me. I got to thinkin,' what if they decided to stay too and I would have to spend eternity dealin' with 'em?"

"People like them don't get a choice."

"What do you mean?" I asked.

"It was love that kept us here. Love for our Mothers." She explained, "But people like Beau and Eddie didn't know what love was. They did things a purpose. They *meant* to harm people. It weren't like an accident or that they just did things from negligence. They was evil. They was gonna really hurt that little girl. And they have done other things in the past that showed how mean and evil they really was. Nope, people like that don't get a choice. They go straight to hell."

I weren't sure what hell was. Alls I knowed about hell was that Mama liked to tell a lot of people to go there. But as long as I would never see Eddie or Beau Rogers again, that was good enough for me.

"Hey, I'll race you to the beach and back." I said.

"Beach nothin' let's go to the moon." Klara exclaimed.

"The Moon? You mean we can actually do that?"

"We're ghost, dummy, we can go anywhere. The universe is the limit."

"But, I thought it never ends." I said.

"Exactly!" Klara said and she was gone again.

Frank's trial was comin' up soon. The newspapers were all over it. What a sensation. I didn't care if Frank fried for my death, even though he had nothin' to do with it. I didn't care how we got rid of Frank, as long as he went away.

Once in a while I would go over to the jailhouse and mess with him. They had him locked up in a little tiny cell all to himself. Other prisoners had threatened to hurt him over what they thought he had done to me. I liked it when Frank was alone. He would be lying on his bunk thinkin' about his life and nasty things about Mama.

One day he was sittin' there and I appeared at the jail as my old self. I walked right up to Frank and said, "Hi Frank."

I'M TIMMY

His eyes got as big as apple pies and he said, "Timothy? Is that you? Boy, you don't know how glad I am to see you. Guard, guard, come quick. It's Timothy. See? I told you I didn't do it.'"

Frank would be whoopin' and hollerin' and the guards would run down to his cell to see what was the matter.

"Look," he'd say. "Look, I told you he was alive."

"What are you talking about?"

"Oh, come on man, don't mess with me. Open up and let me out of here. What are you blind? The boy, Timothy. He's standin' right cheer."

"What are you, nuts?" the guard would say. "There ain't nobody there. You're gonna fry Walker. Just stop tryin' to get out of it."

Then Frank would turn to me and say, "Come on, kid. Say somethin'. Tell the man you're here."

"I'm afraid I can't do that." I'd say. "I was once told not to say nothin' at all. If I do, I might be accused of fightin' and get a whoopin'."

"Look kid, this ain't no game. I need you to tell them you're alive and to let me go."

"What makes you think I'm alive?"

"Well, you're standin' here ain't ya? 'Course you're alive. How could I see you if you weren't"

My eyes got all wide. "You can see me?" I asked.

"Course," Frank said, "Quit screwin' around."

"Can you see me now?" I asked after I disappeared.

"Hey, kid, where'd you go?" Frank looked confused.

"Can you see me now?" I asked after I turned into my dead self.

"Ahhh!" Frank would scream, and I would laugh and laugh.

I liked jumpin' out at Frank and makin' him nervous. He was always on edge. I would wait until he had just fallin' asleep and I would pull his blankets off of his cot. Or I would hover over him and be right in his face when he opened his eyes.

Frank would scream bloody murder.

All of the guards talked about him. Some even had bets going of how much time he'd get or if he'd get the chair. I didn't care either way. As long as he was away from mama and she was safe.

One night while Frank was lying there in the dark I said,

"Hey Frank, guess what? I heard the guards talkin'. Do you know what they're gonna do to you? First, they are goin' to strap you into a hard wooden chair, they will pull the straps real tight. So tight that the blood will stop flowin' through your veins. Then, they will put a black hood over your face and you'll be in total darkness."

Frank's heart began to race. His breathin' sped up like he was runnin' for his life.

"Shut- up, shut-up, shut-up!" He screamed.

"Don't worry, you won't be able to see," I went on, "but your other senses'll take over. You'll be able to hear the tickin' of the clock on the wall. And all the people sittin' there waitin' for 'em to flip the switch. One will scream out, "Burn in hell, Child killer!"

I started to laugh.

"Shut-up, damn you!"

"You'll feel that cold water drippin' over your head, just as they tighten the straps round your chin. Your tongue will feel like it is being squeezed like a zit not quite ready to pop, you'll hear the guard walk over and, CLICK! The volts will buzz like a million flies into your body."

"Shut the hell up!" Frank covered his ears with his hands.

"Do ya think it'll be over then? Oh, no. Here comes the best part. They say you will feel your blood begin to boil as you start to sizzle while all the water comes out your pores. You'll start to shake like bread crumbs in a blender, and your eyes will pop out of their sockets. And flames will fly out of your mouth and your hood will catch fire. Woo hoo! I can't wait to see that! "

I started dancin' all around his cell.

Frank kept his ears covered as he rocked back and forth.

Each day I would go over and have little talks like this with Frank. He got to where he couldn't sleep. He would just sit on his bed and be rockin' back and forth.

One day while I was sittin' there, the guards came to his cell and said, "Walker, you got a visitor."

I wondered who it could be as I went with Frank to the visitors area.

To my surprise it was Mrs. Calhoun.

She looked like her legs had healed up and there was barely a limp at all.

Mrs. Calhoun sat down.

"Hello, Frank." She said.

"Lillian," he nodded.

Suddenly, I was back in time with Frank and Mrs. Calhoun, except they were much younger lookin'. They were sittin' on the high school lawn, talkin' and laughin'. He leaned over and kissed her. Her eyes were filled with love. I saw them dancin' and goin' on picnics, and havin' a time. I even saw them huggin' and kissin' in the back seat of Frank's car. Not the car that mama bought, but a different one. One he must have had when he was in high school.

Then I saw mama. Oh my goodness, she 'bout took my breath away. She was so young and pretty. She looked at Frank in the hallways of the school and I could tell from the way he looked at her, he liked her.

Then I saw Frank with mama doin' all of the things he used to do with Mrs. Calhoun. I saw Mrs. Calhoun sittin' on her bed cryin'. Franks picture was on her nightstand.

Instantly, I was back with them at the jail.

"I hear you're not doing so well," said Mrs. Calhoun.

"Yeah, well, I've been better. What are you doin' here, Lillian?" Frank wanted to know.

"Well, I've come to tell you that I might have some information about Timothy that can prove you didn't have anything to do with his death."

Frank's head perked up.

"What kind of information?"

"Well, maybe he was at the school when it blew up. Maybe he died in the explosion." Mrs. Calhoun whispered.

"What makes you say that?" Frank asked.

T. S. Kincaid

"Well, I had told him that he could go back inside to retrieve his mittens and I can't remember if he came back out or not."

Oooo, Mrs. Calhoun, look at you. I said to myself. You really have changed. I believe you are tryin' to mend your ways.

"I have already talked to the defense lawyer and I've agreed to testify if they think it will help."

"Why are you doin' this? Frank asked.

"I'm just tryin' to right a wrong, that's all."

"Well, thank you." Frank said.

"I'd better be going now. Take care." Said Mrs. Calhoun with a faint smail on her face.

I walked with Mrs. Calhoun to her car. When she got inside I said, "Hi, Mrs. Calhoun."

She 'bout jumped out of her skin. She burst into tears and said, "Oh, please don't hurt me."

"Don't be scared, I'm not gonna hurt you. I just want you to know that I know you're tryin' to do the right thing by helpin' Frank. But it's no use. You see, Frank may not have killed me, but he has done a lot of things he needs to answer for and I'm here to see to it he does. Whether he fries or not don't matter to me. But one way or the other he's gonna pay."

Chapter 18

LIKE I SAID, I quit goin' out with Mama, but after she came home today, I wish I'd kept better watch. She was flutterin' 'round the house all giddy with excitement. She ran to her closet and picked out one dress after the other, throwin' 'em on the floor in a big ole heap. She finally found one she liked best and held it in her arms and started dancin' around singin' *California Here I Come*.

T. S. Kincaid

She ran to the kitchen and picked up the phone and told the operator she would like to make a long-distance, person-to- person call to Robert Pike in Raymond, Mississippi. The only time I ever knowed her to call Uncle Bob was when there was somethin' wrong, but Mama weren't actin' like nothin' was wrong. She was actin' happy.

"Hey, Bob, I wanted you to be the first to know, I'm movin' to L.A. in the next week or two. "

"Why are you movin' to Louisiana?" Asked Bob."

"Not Louisiana, you nit-wit. Los Angeles, California. Oh, Bob I am so happy! I am finally gettin' my big break. My life couldn't be better."

"Now hold on," said Bob, "What are you talkin' about?"

"I'm tellin' you, I finally met someone. He's a big Hollywood producer. He said he had a part that would be perfect for me. So he is comin' back in a couple of weeks to take me there. He said somethin' 'bout havin' to make all the necessary arrangements or somethin' 'fore he can come back to get me."

Mama was talkin' so fast, I had a hard time following what she was sayin'. So, did Uncle Bob cause he kept tellin' her to slow down and say that part again.

I'M TIMMY

He was askin' her things like who exactly this guy was, and where'd they meet, and why would she decide to go to California with some stranger and all kinds of things I wanted to know.

"What about your job?" Bob asked.

That's what I was thinkin'. I's glad Uncle Bob was askin' her all these questions. I hated getting' inside mama's head to find out things. Her thoughts always go in all different directions and I have a hard time keepin' up with her.

"Oh, that ole dump? I quit that place. You didn't think I would stay there forever did ya? Don't ya see. Goin' to Hollywood is my big break. The one I've been waitin' for my whole life. Can't ya just be happy for me?"

I could tell Uncle Bob wanted to be happy, but he sounded more worried than anything.

"I don't know, it sounds awfully fishy to me. You mean some big Hollywood Producer came into the diner and bam! You were discovered?"

"Well, not exactly," said Mama. "I was out at the Moonlight Lounge and happened to bump into him."

"The Moonlight? You mean that old dive off the highway? What would a big Hollywood producer be doin' in there? You think he can be trusted?" Asked Bob.

"Oh! Just forget it. I knew I never should have said nothin' to you! You always try to spoil all of my fun!"

"Look, sis. I'm only tryin' to get the facts here."

The more Uncle Bob talked, the madder Mama got. She finally ended up gettin' so upset she hung the phone up on him.

"Nobody gives a shit about my happiness!" She said right out loud.

I do, Mama. That's all I care about. I reached out to touch her arm.

She shivered and said, "Damn, it's cold in here. I can't wait to get out of this godforsaken' place."

The next mornin' Mama flew out of bed barely makin' it to the bathroom. I thought she had to pee, so I didn't follow her. Then, I heard her, so I went through the door and found her kneeling on the floor by the toilet. Pieces of her supper were in big chunks floatin' in the water. She acted like she was goin' to throw up a few more times, but nothin' came out. She reached for the toilet paper and flushed the toilet as she blew her nose and wiped the string of drool from her mouth.

She lay on the cold floor starin' up at the ceilin' with a blank look on her face for most of the mornin'.

I'm Timmy

She finally crawled back to bed and slept for a while before wakin' up and repeatin' the same thing all over again.

I felt so bad for her. I'd never seen Mama this sick before. Maybe she had a virus, or she ate somethin' that was bad.

She managed to get to the kitchen and find some crackers that were up in the cabinet. She ate them and started feelin' a little better. In fact, she felt better the later it got. By the end of the day she felt fine. She got dressed and called around to see if she could find a ride to the nearest honky-tonk. One of her many men friends came by and picked her up. Off she went like she didn't have a care in the world.

The next mornin' the same thing happened. She was sick as a dog and throwin' up again. Then as the day went on she would feel better again. This happened the rest of the week. Same thing. Sick in the mornin' and feelin' better by evenin'.

At first, I kept thinkin' she was eatin' the wrong thing and wondered why she would do that if she knew it was makin' her so sick. Then I heard it. And I knew what was the matter with mama.

I think she figured it out too cause I heared her in the bathroom screamin' at herself in the mirror. She had taken a hairbrush and threw it at the mirror, breakin' it to pieces. There were a thousand mama's lookin' back at herself in that busted mirror.

She kept sayin' to herself over and over, "Oh! God! This can't be happenin'!' She rocked back and forth on the bathroom floor. I reached out to make her feel better, but she'd just shudder and tuck her legs up close to her body. So, I just left her alone. Maybe she didn't feel good, all that throwin' up and stuff.

When she was finally feelin' better Mama went to the phone and picked it up to see if anyone else was on the line. It was clear, so she called her friend.

"Janet, do you think you can come over? I need someone to talk to and I'm sure Ida Stokes is listenin' in on this line."

"I am not!" Said Ida Stokes.

"See? Janet, do you mind?"

"Course not lovey, I'll be there in a jiffy."

Before long the woman who was Frank's friend came to our door. She was Judy's mom. The woman Frank had at our house and was talkin' to at the gas station the day they found out I was missin'.

I thought Frank said she wasn't a friend of Mamas. 'Course Frank lied about so many things that I guess I shouldn't be surprised by this.

I'm Timmy

"I'm pregnant. Can you believe this shit? Havin' some little ankle- biter crawlin 'around is the last thing I need or want. Do you know anyone who can help me get rid of it?"

Wait. What was she sayin?' Get rid of it? Is she crazy? I'm not real happy about Mama havin' another baby. I am her baby. I am her son. The only person she really needs in her life. But, I don't want to see anything bad happen to this baby. Why would mama want to kill it? I don't understand.

Janet took a cigarette out of the pack and handed one to Mama.

"Just calm down." She said as she went to the ice box and got herself a beer.

"How could you let this happen? I always thought you were smarter than that." Janet said.

"Yeah, me too." Said Mama.

"Who's is it, anyway?" Janet asked.

"How the hell should I know?" Mama stated.

"Maybe you can find yourself another sucker to marry you real quick 'fore anybody finds out. Like you did with Allen." Janet reminded Mama.

What was she sayin'? I think she was tryin' to say that Daddy wasn't my daddy. I was startin' to get real pissed off at this lady.

"Just when my life was finally comin' together, somethin' like this has to go and happen." Cried Mama.

"Oh! I feel for ya, honey. I certainly wouldn't want another kid, especially at your age."

"Just how old do you think I am, Miss Smartass!" yelled Mama.

"Well sweetie, you've got to be pushin' thirty. And you know what they say? The older you get, the harder it is to get that baby fat off."

Mama's face got all red. I could tell she was getting' real mad too. Seemed like this friend of hers was only makin' things worse.

"Well, do you know anyone who can help me or not?" Mama asked.

"I don't know," said Janet. "Maybe. I'll check around and get back with you."

"Well, try to find someone in a hurry. I'm leavin' for California in a few weeks ya know."

"Well, it ain't gonna be cheap, I can tell you that." Janet told her. "You got any money?"

"A little." Mama said. "How much do you think it will cost?"

I couldn't believe Mama was even talkin' about this. Why was she wantin' to kill this life inside of her so bad? She was makin' me so mad, I had to get away

from her for a while. I thought of the school and was
instantly there.

Most of the burnt wood and busted windas was still
there. It looked like a lot of people had been pokin'
around. They was footprints and trash everywhere.
One single door remained standin' and the words KEEP
OUT was written in big black letters across the front of
it. It looked funny standin' there all by itself with
nothin' else around it.

I thought back to that awful day. Suddenly the
walls and building reappeared. The wind was howlin'
outside, rattlin' the windas. I saw myself bangin' on
that icy pane. The memory of the cold rushed back to
me makin' my teeth chatter. I hugged myself with my
now scorched arms.

Then I remembered the fire and the heat from the
flames and the smoke that smothered my lungs. Oh, I
thought I was so clever startin' that fire. I remember
how shocked I was that it had burned so fast.

If only I could go back to that day and forget about
that stupid mitten. I would have made it to the bus and
gone home. Where I should have been. If only Frank

had come for me. If only Mrs. Calhoun had known I had not gotten on that bus. If only. If only.

I was so deep in thought I didn't notice the police officer that was standin' there. It was Steve. Mike was there too, but he was on the other side of the playground. I heard him holler to Steve.

"Hey! I think I got somethin' here." Mike rushed over with it in his hand. Steve looked at it.

It was a shoe. My shoe. They found it. Now maybe Frank will get off.

"Could be anybody's. After all this was a school with lots of children in it. I am sure there must have been extra pairs of shoes lyin' around." Said Steve.

"Should I bag it?" Asked Mike.

"Nah," said Steve. "I don't think it's anything."

"You know, Steve, if I didn't know any better, I'd say you were tryin' to find Frank guilty." Said Mike.

"That piece of shit is guilty." Steve snapped.

"Yeah, but what about what that teacher said? Maybe the kid didn't get on that bus."

"You know that son of a bitch is screwing my wife?" Steve asked.

And your daughter, don't forget your daughter, I said. But I don't think he heard me.

I'M TIMMY

Then I heard Mike say what I just said. Oh, he was thinkin' it. Steve didn't hear him.

"Look, I know the guy is a piece of garbage, but do you really think he deserves to die?" Mike asked.

"You're a married guy right?" Asked Steve.

"Absolutely." Said Mike. "Happily."

"What would you do to keep your wife?" Steve looked him dead in the eye.

"I guess, just about anythin' I had to." Mike said.

Mike said he was gonna go back to where he found the shoe to see if there was anything else he could find.

Steve stood there. He thought about what they just talked about and about how much he hated Frank. I think he hated Frank almost as much as I did. He seemed frustrated. He kicked the ashes and trash with his foot. Something in that mess caught his eye. I followed his eyes to what he was lookin' at. I seen it too. There on the ground was what looked like a small bone with little teeth stickin' out.

Steve picked it up. He looked at it closely and I heard him say in his head it was a jawbone. A jawbone of a person. A young person. A young person who was missin.' A person named Timothy Thomson.

That's right. It was me.

I thought Steve was gonna tell Mike to bring him that bag they put stuff in. But he didn't. He just quietly put my jawbone in his pocket and never said a word.

When I returned to Mama a couple of days had passed. I was still mad at her so I spent some time with Klara.

It was evenin' and mama was walkin' down a long dark alley. Her heels clicked on the red bricks that stuck out unevenly down the thin road. She stopped at a back door at the end of the alleyway and lightly tapped on the door with her gloved hand.

The door opened and she was quickly brought in by a man with red hair, wearin' a white coat. The dimly lit room smelled of puke and old blood. The man asked her if she had the money.

Mama said, "Yes." And handed him a small white envelope. She quickly took off her coat and gloves and threw them into a nearby chair. The man lifted the flap of the envelope and counted the tens and twenties.

"There's only $200 here. I said $250.

"Yes, I know." Said Mama, " I'm real sorry. That was all I could manage. I'll have the rest to you by next week."

I'm Timmy

"I don't give credit!" Barked the man. "What else you got?"

'Nothin', I had to hock my ring to get this."

"Then forget it." Growled the man.

"Oh, please. Can't we think of somethin' else? I'll do anything." Mama eyes looked desperate.

"Anything?" asked the man.

Mama nodded.

The man smiled. "Well then, I 'm sure we can think of somethin'.

The man placed his hand on Mama's neck and she lowered herself to her knees. He unzipped his pants.

I was so sick, I looked away. I was relieved when the man finally groaned and pushed Mama away. She stood up and wiped her mouth on the back of her hand.

"Take off your clothes from the waist down and get up on the table."

The man walked over to some tools on a table as Mama did what he said.

Chill bumps ran down her legs as she slid upon the cold table. She raised her knees into the air and spread her feet apart.

What was she doing?

The man came back to the table with a bunch of hooks and knives that were all rusty. The smell of rust and dirty soap water lingered in the air. The man handed Mama a dingy towel to place under herself.

"Is it gonna hurt?" Mama asked. Her eyes looked worried.

"I can't promise it won't. The towel is for the blood. Try not to drip any on the floor." The man said coldly.

What are they doin'? No! This is why mama came? She's tryin' to get rid of the baby.

I won't let you do this, Mama.

Mama laid back on the table and took a deep breath.

I knocked the tray over. The knives and hooks fell and bounced all over the floor. The man in the white coat jumped.

"What is the meaning of this?" He yelled.

Mama looked scared to death.

The man bent over to get the tool with the long hook and I kept slidin' it across the floor just out of reach.

"What the hell's going on here?" the man hollered.

I picked up one of the knives and sliced his hand with it. He gasped and grabbed a towel and wrapped his hand. The blood soaked it within a matter of seconds.

I'm Timmy

"Something screwy is going on here lady, and I don't want any part of it."

"Please, wait! I'll pay you double. I'll have the money by tomorrow."

The man looked like he was thinking about it. He went to pick up his tools again and I was so mad I appeared as my dead self in his face.

"Get the hell away from my mother!" I screamed as loud as I could.

"Forget it lady, get your damn clothes on."

The guy grabbed the envelope from his desk and ran out the door.

"Wait!" Cried Mama. "You promised. Where the hell are you goin?' Come back. Hey, what about my money?"

He was at the end of the alley before Mama could put her clothes back on. By the time she got to the door he was long gone.

Mama stumbled back down the alley and made it to a car just as a woman who had driven her there opened the car door.

"Oh, honey, have you finished already?" The woman asked.

"No! That bastard took my money and ran off with it. Oh! I am so pissed I don't know what to do!" Screamed Mama.

"Well, we'll go to the police." Said the lady.

"And tell them what? Excuse me officer, I just tried to have an illegal abortion and the doctor ran off with my money before I could get the job done. Yeah, that's gonna go over real well."

"Well?" asked the lady. "What are ya gonna do now?"

"Just take me home. I'll find some way to get rid of this baby."

I rode all the way back with Mama. The more she talked the angrier I got. What is wrong with you, Mama? What happened to the mother I know and love?

When we pulled into the driveway, Mama's friend asked her if she wanted her to stay. Mama told her there was no need and thanks for everything anyway.

She watched her friend drive away as she turned the key to the door. There were tears in her eyes as she walked over to the ice box to get herself a beer.

She kicked off her shoes and plopped down on the couch bending forward to grab a cigarette from the coffee table. Big rings of smoke circled her head as she sipped her beer.

I'm Timmy

"This is just great!" Mama said, "What the hell am I gonna do now?"

She's just upset. Once she gets some sleep, she will feel better and then we can work this out.

Out of nowhere Mama stood up and started beating herself in the stomach. Over and over she hit herself screaming, "Damn you! I'll get rid of you one way or the other!"

Before I realized what was happenin,' I grabbed Mama's arm and threw her back down on the couch. I was so angry I appeared as my dead self. Mama gasped and screamed.

"Mama!" I yelled. "What are you doin? Why are you tryin to kill this baby.?"

"Get away from me!" She screamed as she threw her fists through me. "Get away, you hear?"

"But Mama," I tried to say as calmly as possible. "Why would you want to kill this baby? Don't you love it?"

"Love it? Hell no, I don't love it. I hate children!! I always have. I'm glad you're dead!"

"Stop, Mama! Don't go too far!" I yelled.

"I never wanted you either! I am so, so glad you are gone. Now go back to where-ever you came from and take this little bastard with you!"

"Nooooo!" I screamed! I have never been so angry at Mama. I guess Klara was right, I had to get good and mad for Mama to hear me.

"I stayed here for you, you bitch! I gave up eternity with Daddy! I stayed here for you!"

"Well, you shouldn't have! I never loved you. You were like an infection I couldn't get rid of. When I thought that Frank killed you, that was even better. I could get rid of both of you and I didn't have to lift a damn finger."

I was stunned.

I flew around the room tearin' up everything I could find. I threw plates and furniture. I screamed and yelled. I thought of all of the awful things Mama had ever done to me and knew now she would surely have to pay.

This went on for what seemed like hours.

"I didn't ask to be born!" I yelled at her.

"Well, if it had been up to me, you wouldn't have been. I tried my damnedest with you too, but you were always so strong. You'd just go with the flow. Never gettin' angry. Always, I love you, Mama. How pathetic!"

I grabbed Mama by the hair of the head. I put my face directly in hers and said, "Now you listen to me

I'M TIMMY

Mama, and you listen good. I am here whether you like it or not. I am not going to let you hurt this baby, do you hear me? I will be with you ALWAYS. Watching, and makin' sure you are takin' care of her and doin' right by her. You are goin' to raise this baby the best way you can, and you are not goin' to ever try to hurt her again, you understand?"

Mama was shakin' and cowerin' in the corner.

There was a loud knock on the door. Boom, boom, boom! They knocked again. Then the door burst open. It was two officers. Their red patrol lights were flashing behind them as they stood in the door way. One reached over and flipped the switch for the lights, but they wouldn't come on. He pulled out his flashlight and found a lamp on the floor. It had become unplugged during all of my rantin' and ravin'.

The officer plugged the light back in and found Mama curled up like a baby in the corner.

"Ma'am? Are you alright? We got a call there was a disturbance here."

"Shhh," Whispered Mama. "I just got him to quiet down. Please, don't make him angry."

The officer looked around. Finally, after not seein' anyone he said, "Who?"

"What do you mean who? My boy, he's right here."

The officers looked at each other.

Mama started laughin' and screamin' hysterically.

"He's fooled you too. What's wrong, can't you see him? He's standin right cheer." Mama was gettin' more and more upset."

"Simmer down, lady. Hey, Jack?" One officer said to the other, " I thought I recognized this address. This is Frank Walker's place. You know? That kid he murdered. This is that kids mother. She must think she's talking to her dead son."

"Call an ambulance, this one's goin' to the looney-bin." Said Jack.

Mama was still laughing and screamin' like she was head cheerleader at the Homecoming.

Mama put her hands out.

"Here, take me away," she said. "Take me somewhere he can't get me. I made him angry, you see. He's been here all along, the little bastard. Watchin' me . I thought he was here, but tonight was the first time he showed himself. He looks hideous. Frank really did a number on him. Can't you see?"

Mama kept on talkin' til the ambulance finally arrived. They gave her a shot which calmed her down. By the time she got to the hospital, she was calmer but still talkin' about me and her trip to California.

I'M TIMMY

I waited with her while she slept. It was a long night. I had a lot of time to think. How could I have been so blind? All this time I had been under Mama's spell, just like other people, especially men in her life. I thought she loved me. But she proved tonight she never did.

Oh Daddy! Why didn't I listen to you? Come back. Can't you please come back and get me? Our talk replayed in my head. *Come now, son or you will be here forever.* Eternity is a long, long time.

By mornin' the doctors came in to see mama and not much about the way she had acted had changed. Uncle Bob was with them. He said he drove through the night sos he could be here.

Mama didn't even act like she knew who he was.

"You see, Mr. Pike, I'm afraid your sister has suffered what we call a psychotic break. Right now she is living in a dream world. She truly believes she sees her son. All of this is understandable considering all she has been through and her fragile mental state." Explained the doctor.

"How long do you think she will have to be here?" asked Uncle Bob.

"Well, that's why I called you. We need to discuss a long- term plan. It could be months, or even years.

We just don't know much about this type of illness. We also need to know if there is any way you could make arrangements to take the baby."

"The baby? Oh, of course. Well, that is something I will have to speak with my wife about. I will certainly let you know one way or the other. Do you think the baby will be alright? I mean with my sister in her condition and all?"

"Oh yes, the baby will be perfectly fine. At least she is in a place where we can see to it she is well taking care of and given the proper nutrition for the baby. From the looks of how she tried to harm herself, she is lucky to still be pregnant. That was another reason we will have to insist she stay here. We can't have her being a danger to herself and others."

Uncle Bob sat with Mama for the rest of the day. He tried to talk to her, but she was so out of it. He even held her hand and cried a time or two. I think Uncle Bob is a good man. Even if he did hit me that one time. But Uncle Bob is not the problem. I don't want my sister bein' raised by the likes of Erma.

After getting a good nights sleep in the hotel, Uncle Bob headed home. I could read his mind and tell he was really dreadin' talkin' to Aunt Erma.

"Are you out of your mind?" Erma Shrieked. "What on earth were you thinkin? Even considerin' takin' a baby from some crazy nut like your sister? No way! I ain't doin' it!"

"I just thought you might consider it. The poor little thing will have no place to go after birth."

"They have orphanages, don't they?" Erma smirked. "Let it go to one of those."

That was the end of the conversation. Uncle Bob didn't put up a fight and Erma won as usual. I was so mad that I tripped Aunt Erma as she was walkin' into the kitchen, causin' her to fall into the doorway and give herself a bloody nose.

I stayed with Mama off and on for the next few weeks. Not for Mama's sake, but for hers, my sisters.

Every once and a while I'd drop in on Frank's trial just to see how things was goin'. I have to tell you, I was worried there for a while that they weren't gonna find him guilty on account of not havin' a body.

Nobody took into account what Mrs. Calhoun said cause there weren't any evidence to prove otherwise. I guess there was a hole in Steve's pocket and my jawbone somehow disappeared.

T. S. Kincaid

Anyways after a few weeks they did find him guilty and the judge did give him a death sentence. I was happy with that, but I wanted to be there to make sure things was done right. Like I said, before I ain't got nothin' but time.

Chapter 19

FRANK DIED TODAY.

It weren't like you or me thought though. I stayed all night in his cell remindin' him of the visitor he had earlier that day. It was Steve. They sat in the visitor's area talkin'. Frank was surprised to see him there, me too.

"What are you doin' here? Come to sulk 'cause I may get a stay from the governor?"

T. S. Kincaid

"What makes you think that?' Asked Steve.

"You know you ain't got no body. Leaves a little doubt, don't ya think?"

"You're not going to be getting a stay." Said Steve.

"Oh, we'll see." Frank smirked.

"Listen to me you bastard, you can wipe that shit eatin' grin off of your face. I know you've been screwing my wife. And I just found out about Judy today. You won't be getting a stay."

"Hey, at least I'm keepin' it in the family. Sides you can't execute a guy for screwin' another man's wife. Or daughter for that matter."

"You're right." Steve admitted.

Frank smiled again.

"But I did happen to mention to the governor that little incident that happened a few months back to that couple over in Lincoln county."

Frank's face turned white.

His thoughts immediately went to that night.

He was again down by a river with another girl in his car. The girl looked frightened and worried.

"Look Officer," she said. "I just wanted you to give me a ride home. I don't know what we're doin' here."

"Take it easy, honey. I just wanted to talk for a while. Now just relax." Said Frank.

He started pullin' the girl closer to him and tryin' to kiss her. She kept pushin' him away.

"Please, just take me home." She started crying.

"Come on now, give me a kiss." Frank forced his tongue into her mouth.

She slapped him.

Frank got so mad that he started chokin' that girl. And I mean chokin' her hard.

She kicked and tried to get away, but he was too strong. I wanted to stop him, but this was somethin' that's already happened and alls I could do was watch.

The girl passed out. Frank quickly lifted up her skirt and pulled down her underpants. He was just finishin' doin' what he was doin' to her, when a car pulled up.

A young man got out of his car and ran over and opened the door to Frank's patrol car.

"You son of a bitch, get away from my girl!"

"Look, boy, just calm down." Frank said. "I think she's sick or something. Here I'll help you get her into your car, and you can take her home."

Frank pulled the girls limp body out of the patrol car and carried her over and placed her in the young man's car.

The young man quickly got into his car and started tryin' to talk to his girlfriend.

"Jenny? Jenny honey, what's wrong."

The young man started to shake her. Her body only moved when he nudged her.

The young man started screamin' at Frank. "What did you do? What did you do? I'll kill you, you son of a bitch."

The young man lunged at Frank and boom!

His body flew back into the driver's seat of his car. The young man lay there with his head in his girlfriend's lap. Frank smoked a cigarette and waited while the young man bled out.

Frank got on his radio and called it in. When his fellow police officers arrived, this is the lie he told.

"I was doin' my patrol when I come across this couple parked here by the river. I could see they were struggling or havin' some sort of fight. When I got out and approached the car, I saw that the young lady was passed out. I asked what happened and the young man said, she was just sleepin'. Upon further inspection I saw the young lady was deceased. I drew my gun and told the suspect to step out of the car. When he did, he lunged at me and I had no choice, but to shoot him."

"You thought you got away with it didn't you?" Asked Steve.

Yes, thought Frank, I did.

"Well, asshole, turns out the girl lived. We've been keepin' it under wraps. Why the hell do you think you were put on suspension anyway? It takes more than screwin' my wife. So you see, all it took was one phone call to the governor and I reminded him that you were the officer that was first at the scene the night his nephew died."

Frank wasn't grinning or smiling no more.

Steve waited until they took Frank back to his cell.

"Ooo, you are gonna fry for sure. I knew you were evil the from the first time I saw you!" I taunted. "Hey Frank, I don't know if you can hear 'em or not, but there's all kinds of people gatherin' outside holdin' up signs and dancin' around sayin' they're gettin' ready for a Bar-b-que." I laughed and laughed.

Franks execution wasn't scheduled until later that mornin' so I decided to go to the park and see Klara for a while.

When I got back to the prison, I heard the news. You know what that crazy Frank done? He took off his pants and ripped them to shreds. Then he tied all the shreds together and made himself a rope.

They found him with that rope tide around his neck so tight they couldn't hardly cut if off. He'd been dead quite a while before anybody found him.

I was so mad! I wanted him to suffer. But I guess I should have known how much Frank liked to be in charge. He didn't want to do anything that would make me happy. I guess all and all I should just be glad he's gone and I'll never have to deal with him again.

I went and checked on Mama, now that Frank was dead. I don't think anybody told her, cause if they did she didn't act like she woulda understood. She was sittin' in the corner of her room brushin' her hair sayin' "Who's a pretty girl? I'm a pretty girl." Then she would laugh like crazy.

At least Mama weren't hurtin' herself or the baby. She mostly just sat like the way she was now all the time. I think the baby will be safe, but I will keep an eye out just in case.

I did a lot of thinkin' while I was sittin' there with Mama.

I thought about Frank. And what hell must be like for him, and if he'd seen Eddie and Beau since they was all there together. I thought about mama and wished she weren't like she is now. I know I am partly to blame scaring her like I did, but at the time I didn't know what else to do.

I thought about daddy. I wondered where he was. I wondered if he could hear me and knew all of this was happenin' or if he had just gone on and we were all forgotten. He said, he wasn't supposed to be here when he came for me. I wondered if he got in any kind of trouble for that and if he'd ever risk comin' back again.

I thought of Klara, and how long she has been here and how much longer we both still have to go.

I thought of Mrs. Calhoun, and wondered if she still felt guilty. After all, she tried to help Frank. A man she once loved and now hated. I wondered if she cried when she heard the news about Frank.

I thought of Aunt Erma and wondered how she ever got to be so spiteful. Aunt Erma wasn't evil, she was just mean. And her son Larry was going to be just like her, and I felt sorry for Uncle Bob.

Then I thought of someone who completely slipped my mind. I don't know how that could have happened. I guess all of this hatred and revenge had clouded my thoughts and wouldn't let me remember. But now I did. I thought of the one person who truly loved me, besides daddy, Mawmaw Pike.

T. S. Kincaid

I went back to her old house she sold. I roamed through all of the rooms rememberin' all the good times we had. I went and sat on the porch swing and began swingin'. I did like Klara did, and let the folks now livin' there believe it was the wind a swingin' that swing, even though there weren't none.

I closed my eyes and concentrated real hard. I saw a sign that read, Waverton Hills. Instantly, I was there.

Chapter 20

I STOOD IN the middle of that dimly lit hospital room, not revealin' myself. There was an old woman lyin' in a dingy hospital bed. The room smelled like someone had had an accident and it weren't just that they'd peed. As I got closer, I heard the old woman say, "Timmy? Timmy? Where are you child?"

I stood there confused.

T. S. Kincaid

A woman in a white nurse's uniform quickly came into the room.

"Oh, shut up old woman. Your precious Timmy isn't here. Keep quiet or I will have to tie you down again."

No way. It couldn't be. Was this my Mawmaw Pike? I got closer and could see her silver hair was all matted to the bed. She had crumbs of caked food on her mouth and it looked like she had not had a bath in weeks. I could feel how her she felt. My mouth was so dry, I could blow dust from it.

"Please," begged my Mawmaw. "Please, can I have a drink of water?"

"I told you the last time you asked. No more water for you. Your have already pissed yourself once today. Haven't you learned your lesson? Water just makes you pee the bed, and I'll be damned if I am goin' to clean up after you!"

I could feel the rage running through my veins. I grabbed the woman by the hair of the head and screamed in her face, "Listen, Bitch! Get her a damn drink of water!"

I pulled her by her hair all the way over to the sink and slammed her face up against the mirror. I grabbed her hand and forced her to take a cup and fill it with water. I led her back over to my mawmaw, and made her gently hand her the cup.

My grip was strong on her arm and she started twistin' and strugglin' to get away. I held her arm even tighter.

She started screamin', "Somebody help me! Help me!"

I tightened my grip even more and led her over to the winda. I pulled back the curtain, and slid the winda up. Light filled the room and fresh air blew in, chasin' that awful odor away.

I held her in that opened winda with her body halfways in and halfways out. She was screamin' but no one could see me, so she looked like she was tryin' to jump.

"TIMOTHY, NO!" Mawmaw shouted. "No, don't hurt her. You are a good boy. Bring her back in child."

I looked over at Mawmaw and saw the scared look in her eyes.

"Please, honey, you are a good boy, leave the lady alone."

"Mawmaw, you can see me? How is that possible?" I didn't reveal myself so I was confused. Then I remembered somethin' that Klara once told me.

T. S. Kincaid

They can only see you if you yell, or get good and mad, OR if they're close to dying themselves.

I looked at mawmaw again, and saw the sadness in her eyes. I pulled the nurse back into the room away from the winda and slung her across the floor. She jumped up and took off runnin' so fast. I could hear her screamin' as she ran down the three flights of stairs and out the front door. She screamed all the way to her car. As she was about to get in it and drive away, two men in white coats grabbed her. She kicked and screamed and fought all the way back into the hospital. After they gave her a shot she finally calmed down.

She asked if she could leave, but they told her they wanted her to stay for a few days, just to make sure she was alright. They put her in the room right below mawmaws.

"Thank you, Timmy. Where have you been? Come here and let me get a good look at you."

I was so ashamed. I knew how I looked and I didn't want mawmaw to see me that way, but you know what? She didn't see how scary-lookin I was, she only saw me the way I used to look. The way I looked when I was livin' in the old house with her. She smiled at me.

"Come here, honey, and let me see you better. My sweet boy, you were dealt a terrible hand in life. I don't know what happened to you, but I am glad you are here with me now. I have missed you, and I love you."

My heart melted. All of the hatred that I felt for so long seemed to float away.

It felt so good to finally be with someone who truly loved me.

Another nurse came in to check on mawmaw. Mawmaw's eyes lit up when she entered the room.

"Oh, my goodness Miss Pike, you certainly look a mess. I am so sorry, you have had to deal with that nasty Miss Watkins. If I had known she was going to be so neglectful, I never would have recommended she take my shifts.

"How was the weddin?" Mawmaw asked.

"Oh, it was wonderful, Jim and I went to Mammoth Cave for our honeymoon."

The nurse gently wiped Mawmaw's mouth and helped her get in her chair beside her bed.

"Oh, really? That's where my Louis and I went. I loved it there."

I noticed the sparkle in her eyes. Mawmaw had that same sparkle every time she talked about Pawpaw Pike.

The nurse quickly changed the sheets on mawmaw's bed. Then, she went into the bathroom and turned on the shower. She took a chair and placed it in the shower for mawmaw to sit on.

When mawmaw stood up, I seen the sores on her back from where she'd been layin' in the bed for so long. That sure did bother me and made me so mad.

"Mawmaw," I said, "I think I'm gonna take a look around."

"Of course, dear, I'll see you later." Said Mawmaw.

"Who ya talking to, Miss Pike?" Asked the sweet nurse.

"Oh, excuse me for bein' so rude, this heres my grandson, Timmy. Timmy, this is Miss Jones."

"It's McIntire now," the nurse reminded mawmaw.

"Hello, Timmy, It's nice to meet you."

I could tell she was just puttin' on for mawmaw's sake, cause I weren't standin' anywheres near where she was lookin'.

I decided to go downstairs and visit Nurse Watkins. She was sleepin'. I tried to wake her but she wouldn't budge. I guess what they knocked her out with was some mighty powerful stuff.

Next, I decided to go outside. They didn't have no swings, but there was a nice bench to sit on. I sat there for a while listenin' to all of the different birds. There was a robin sittin' up in her nest and I could hear her babies. I also heard the cardinal, the blue jay and mawmaw's favorite, the meadow lark. They have such a pretty sound.

I sat there listenin' and then I heard a new sound. It was familiar, but one I'd not heard for a long time. It sounded like a little bell. Was I dreamin'? Could it be possible?

I looked 'round and there hangin' from a tree was a windchime. Darn, I thought it was somethin' else. Wait. There it is again, and this was not a windchime. It *was* a bell. My eyes began searchin'. I heard it again, louder this time. Just over there by that big oak tree.

"Dumplin? Is that you?'

I heard that sweet familiar meow. She turned and looked at me. She tilted her head and I swear it seemed like she was thinkin' the same thing I was. She slowly came over to me like a hunter stalkin' it prey. Just takin' her time, in case she was wrong.

But she weren't wrong, and neither was I.

"Dumplin' look at you. You're a sight!"

She ran to me and rubbed her soft body against my legs.

"Where you been girl?" I asked.

"Lookin' for you," she said.

" Wait, what? You can actually talk?"

She looked at me again. Her mouth wasn't movin' but I swear I could hear every word she was thinkin'.

"What happened, where did you go?"

Instantly, I was back to that awful night that mama and mawmaw had that fight about sellin' the house and movin'. I saw mama slam the door and run out to get in the car. She threw the car in reverse so fast no one had time to think, much less move. I saw her hit Dumplin'. Dumplin' was thrown over into the weeds. She was injured but not enough to die just yet. She lay there all night. Hopin' I would come and find her. She passed away, just as the sun was comin' up, and she could hear me callin' for her. She knew I had not betrayed her. Her love for me, just like my love for mama, is what caused her to stay.

"But where have you been all this time?" I repeated.

Like me, she had a kind of hatred in her heart that just wouldn't let go. She was angry she had died and I was not able to see or hear her, so she went off on her own for a while. Then she thought of me again, and this time her thoughts led her here to me.

Some place where we can both be loved and be together for all eternity. We were finally home. Oh, I'm not talkin' bout a physical place, but a place where we both could be loved and wanted. Why, we could be home no matter where we was 'cause now we had each other.

I went back up to nurse Watkins room. I heard they was gonna be lettin' her go home in a couple of days. Each time she went to get a drink, I moved it just out of reach. Her throat got so parched she couldn't stand it. I'd let her finally get a sip then spill the whole glass all over her. I knowed it was wrong, but I wanted her to feel the way she made my Mawmaw feel.

She was supposed to be carin' for her, not makin' her last days miserable. I spent the next couple of nights talkin' to her in her dreams. She seemed to get the message and in her dreams I saw her become kinder and more of the nurse she was supposed to be. On the day she was to be discharged, she stood in the doorway of mawmaw's room.

She stood there, her knees knockin'. "Excuse me, Miss Pike?" She finally said.

Mawmaw looked towards her door and said, "Yes, come in."

"I'll stand here if that's okay?" said Nurse Watkins. Her eyes were lookin' all around, checkin' every corner. "I just wanted to tell you how truly sorry I am for the way I treated you. It was very wrong and I hope you can forgive me."

Mawmaw looked over at me and gave me a wink.

"Well, that's real nice of you to come and tell me that. You're forgiven."

Nurse Watkins let out a deep breath.

"Thank you, Ma'am. I'll be going now."

"All right dear, you take care."

With that Nurse Watkins was gone and I knew she would be a better nurse from now on.

Nurse McIntire really surprised me one day. She came in with a ball. At first I couldn't believe it. Nobody ever gave me nothin' so when she held it up and said it was for me I didn't know how to react. She put it on the floor and said I could play with it anytime I wanted.

You better believe I did. I sat in the hallway and bounced it against the walls. That's when all kinds of rumors spread that mawmaw's room was haunted. I even had Klarah come over a time or two and we played and laughed and scared all the other nurses half to death. It was all in fun though. No one acted like Miss

I'M TIMMY

Watkins.   They would just simply say, 'Oh, that's just Timmy."

I knew it was near Mawmaw's time to go.   We spent hours together playin' cards and talkin' about when I was little and she was little.   We talked about how she met Pawpaw and their life together.

I loved how her eyes lit up when she talked about him.   She was so pretty sittin' there with Mama's eyes and the smile on her face.

"Mawmaw, there is somethin' I just gotta ask ya?"

"What is it child?" Mawmaw asked.

"Why is my mama so mean?" I was kind of scared to ask her at first cause I know we ain't supposed to talk about our mother's that way.   But it was somethin' that had been on my mind for a long time and I figured now was as good a time as any.

"Well, child." Mawmaw started.

She didn't   sound mad like I thought she'd be. Really, she sounded kind of sad.

"You see, Timmy, I reckon it's just as much mine and your pawpaw's fault as it is your Mothers. When your mama was a little girl, she was your pawpaw's favorite. In his eyes she could do no wrong. He treated her just like a princess and me like a queen. We both

307

gave her anythin' and everythin' she ever wanted. In other words, we spoiled her to death."

I sat listenin' real close.

"Then when your pawpaw died, it nearly killed her. She cried for days. She didn't even want me to bury him. When I finally did, she would just go to his gravesite a lay on his grave and cry her eyes out. She even said she wanted to crawl down in there with him and die herself. She begged for him to come back. Course, he never did. Then she became angry, not just at me, but God and everybody.

She spent her whole life tryin' to find someone who would treat her the way her daddy did. That's when she met your daddy. He was so good to her. But then you were born."

"But, seems like me bein' there would make her happy." I said.

"No, honey, for you it was just the opposite. She was so jealous of the attention you got, that she couldn't stand it. It was wrong the way she treated you. She grew up never caring for or thinkin' about anybody but herself. I'm sorry, child. Your pawpaw and I should have done better."

I didn't know what to say about that. All I knowed was, like daddy said, some people need to be made accountable for the way they act and that maybe Mama coulda done better if she'd wanted to.

Then, before I knowed it, the time was here. Mawmaw sat in her bed. She looked beautiful. Mrs. McIntire gave her a good bath and combed her hair.

Mawmaw looked me dead in the eye and said, " Timmy, I've made a decision. I can't stand the thought of you stayin' here all be yourself. So, I've decided to stay."

"Mawmaw," I said. "I know that you love me and that you think you know what you are sayin', but there is no way I could let you stay. Pawpaw's waitin' for you. He is so happy that you'll be joinin' him. He's waited a long time, you know? You wouldn't want to disappoint him now would you? Just think, Mawmaw, you will be young again, and you won't have anymore pain. You and pawpaw can spend the rest of eternity in peace. You ain't gotta worry 'bout me. I'll be fine. Sides, I have Dumplin' and Klara to keep me company."

I could tell Mawmaw was gettin' real tired. Then I saw him. It was pawpaw, standin' in the doorway. He reached his hand out for her and she touched his.

"You done good, Timmy" Pawpaw said.

And with that they was gone.

T. S. Kincaid

I sat there once more feelin' empty. But I meant what I said. I did have Dumplin' and Klara and I knew I would be alright.

I decided to go to Mama. She would need someone at a time like this. She was still in her own little world. That was best, I guess. At least she was gettin' good food to eat and bein' looked after while she was carryin' the baby.

I knew now what my purpose would be. I would stay here and take care of my sister, and hers, and theirs. For as long as I was needed.

Alls I can say is heaven help anyone who tries to hurt any of them.

I'm Timmy

A Note from the Author

Dear Reader,

Thank you for selecting this first in a series, I'm Timmy. I must say it was a labor of love and I hope you enjoyed reading it as much as I liked writing it. If you found it interesting and would like to read other books of mine, please contact me at

www.tskincaid.com

I would like to invite you to sign up for my VIP Readers club where you can get the latest news, member only exclusives and book samples.

I look forward to hearing from you soon.

With love,

T. S. Kincaid